THE FOUR BEST THINGS TO DO WHILE SLEEPWALKING

by Suze Charles:

1) Housework. It never gets done while I'm awake.

2) Exercise. See previous explanation.

3) Write my annual Christmas letter. See above.

4) Drink prune juice. At least I'll never remember it happened.

THE FOUR WORST THINGS TO DO WHILE SLEEPWALKING

1) Eat everything in the refrigerator with a teaspoon, including the mayonnaise.

2) Visit with brand-new phone friends in Latin America.

3) Change the oil in my car. (I don't know how to do it while I'm awake, so I certainly don't know why I think I can do it while I'm asleep.)

4) E-mail my senators, encouraging them to pass a law saying all cover models must weigh at least 150 pounds.

Books by Judy Baer

Love Inspired

Be My Neat-Heart #347
Mirror, Mirror #399
Sleeping Beauty #415

Steeple Hill Single Title

The Whitney Chronicles
Million Dollar Dilemma
Norah's Ark

JUDY BAER

"Angel" Award-winning author and three-time RITA®
Award finalist Judy Baer has written more than
seventy books in the past twenty years, including the
bestselling Cedar River Daydreams series, with over
1.25 million copies in print. Her most recent Steeple
Hill Single Title book was *The Baby Chronicles,*
published in September 2007. A native of North Dakota
and graduate of Concordia College in Minnesota, she
currently lives near Minneapolis. In addition to writing,
Judy works as a personal life coach and writing coach.
Judy speaks in schools, churches, libraries, at women's
groups and at writers' workshops across the country.
She enjoys time with her husband, two daughters, three
stepchildren and the growing number of spouses, pets
and babies they bring home. Judy, who once raised
buffalo, now raises horses. Readers are invited to visit
her Web site at www.judykbaer.com.

Sleeping Beauty
Judy Baer

Steeple
Hill®

Published by Steeple Hill Books™

STEEPLE HILL BOOKS

Steeple
Hill®

ISBN-13: 978-0-373-81329-2
ISBN-10:   0-373-81329-5

SLEEPING BEAUTY

www.SteepleHill.com

Printed in U.S.A.

Come to me, all who labor and are heavy laden,
and I will give you rest.
—*Matthew* 11:28

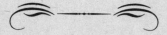

For Joan Marlow Golan—you are one of the best!

Chapter One

My sister, Mickey, apologizes a lot these days.

"I can't imagine what Tommy and Terry were doing to knock it off the top of your china cabinet. You have no idea how badly I feel, Suze. We'll pay for it, of course...."

"Never mind, I didn't like those Waterford crystal candlesticks much anyway."

Mickey has been asking for forgiveness, expressing regret and acting contrite for three years. That's when her twins learned to walk. Before that, life was relatively calm. Since the boys mastered locomotion, however, nothing has been the same. Tommy and Terry are adorable with loose black curls, blue-violet eyes with long lashes as dark as midnight, rosy cheeks and wide smiles that reveal faint dimples. We lovingly refer to them as the Terror

Twins, Tommy Tomahawk and Terry the Tormentor.

Mickey, whose name is short for Michelle, flung herself onto my couch. "I can't go. It would be cruel and unusual punishment to make you take care of the boys for three months."

"Nonsense. They're my flesh and blood. Of course I'll take care of them." Saying it, I felt a little like the martyr Stephen stepping up to be stoned. "Do what you need to do to adopt your baby girl. If it means staying in South America for ten or twelve weeks until the baby is ready to leave the country, then go for it."

Medical problems had made it impossible for Mickey to have any more children, and she's always dreamed of having a little girl. I love my sister and would do anything for her. I'd give her a kidney. Of course, offering to care for the Terrors for twelve weeks might be more like giving her *both* my kidneys.

"Have you heard anything on the new job yet?" Mickey asked.

"I'm interviewing in Chicago on Thursday."

"You aren't moving there are you?"

"No, but I have to interview at the main office."

"What if you have to start immediately? You

wouldn't be able to take care of the kids while we're gone."

"The position doesn't actually open up for four months. Someone is retiring. Besides, if I did have to travel, Mom and Dad could manage an overnight or two with the boys." My parents, though only in their early sixties, can't handle the boys full-time. When I think about it, no one can, not even the boys' own parents. "Mom and Dad would come here to feed the animals anyway."

"Speaking of the animals, what have you got now? Other than that crazed hamster, I mean."

"He's not crazed. He's sensitive, that's all." Whenever Hammie perceives that I'm upset, *he* gets upset, too—and begins to run on that wheel of his until I settle down. He's become a great predictor of my emotions. He's also made my home a much calmer place. I have to stay calm—deep breathing and envisioning a sunny place with vast white beaches and dolphins playing in the surf—otherwise the sound of that whirring, rattling wheel in his cage would drive me nuts.

"There's a lady in my spinning class who was very interested in what you do. She is looking for a dog for her mother—something loving and easy to spoil."

"Chipper would be perfect. She'd like a black Pekingese. He's small, dignified, affectionate, a real character. He needs lots of brushing though."

"That's fine. Her children have requested that Grandma get a dog to groom so she'll be too busy to tell them to cut their hair and dye it back to normal colors. But what's this dog's *problem?*"

All my pets come with problems. I'm a foster mother for a last-chance pet adoption agency. These are the animals that literally no one wants. When they reach our agency, these are the saddest little creatures on the planet. Health problems, age, bad hair and bad habits bring them to us. I take in these pitiful little creatures, fatten them up, doctor them until they are healthy, teach them manners and make them more desirable in any way I can. Then I attempt to place them in loving homes.

"His foot is missing. Got it caught in a mousetrap. He wandered around lost, dragging it until it got infected. It may bother someone else but it doesn't bother Chipper."

Mickey winced. "Poor little thing. Do you have a photo? I'll take it to spinning tomorrow."

At that moment, the mini-watchdog in question set up a commotion in the kitchen. There were no burglars in the house, just two naughty scamps trying to remove a package of Oreos from the top shelf of a cupboard.

Terry stood on my kitchen counter tippy-toed on the Minneapolis telephone book reaching for the cookies while Tommy, belly down on the counter, resolutely held on to Terry's ankles. When Terry fell he'd take Tommy right off the counter with him, but they hadn't factored that into their equation. The twins always assume they will succeed at their schemes and spend little time dwelling on the consequences of their actions.

"Terry!" Mickey screeched unhelpfully. Her guilty son turned to look at her and teetered on his perch. Mickey reached out to catch Terry while I dove for Tommy, still clinging tenaciously to his brother's feet. The impact of Terry's fall sent Mickey flying backward into my kitchen table. I heard the tinkle of breaking glass.

Mickey and Terry stared down at the other Waterford candlestick holder lying shattered on the kitchen floor.

"Oh, well," I said weakly. "At least now they're a matching set again."

Discipline is always harder on the adults than the children themselves. As the boys sat in opposite corners of my living room howling at the indignity of having to stay in one place for more than twelve seconds, Mickey and I sat across the room pretending we could hear ourselves talking.

"Are you going to be able to handle a third child, Mickey?" I tried to be gentle. "It takes a village to raise just these two."

"We'll be fine. The boys will be in school soon. That will help."

It will help Mickey, but what about the American educational system? Isn't it in enough trouble as it is?

"Tell me more about this job interview," Mickey encouraged. "Are you flying in and out the same day?"

"No. The interview is early in the morning. I've made a reservation at the Omni. I'll have dinner, relax and get a good night's sleep to be sharp for the meeting."

"Overnight?" Mickey's blue eyes darkened. "Suze, are you sure?"

"Positive," I said shortly.

"But your problem…What are you going to do about that? I mean, really, a *hotel?*"

I willed myself to be calm. "My 'problem' as you so obliquely refer to it, has kept me from traveling for far too long. I've decided to fight back.

"I'm not going to let it stop me from getting a promotion in my company or from traveling to places I've always wanted to visit. It's war this time, Mickey."

But how to conduct a war with an enemy that only attacks at night while I'm asleep?

"You know how you are, Suze. What if you sleepwalk? You could walk out of the hotel and get into trouble."

Sleepwalking. Who would believe the heartache it has caused me?

"The registration desk at the Omni is not on street level. That's why I chose it. Besides, I bought this." I held up the padlock I'd purchased this morning. "There's no way I'll be able to unlock it if I am asleep. Don't worry. I'll be fine."

My family's tales about the crazy things I've done while sleepwalking are legendary. If I remained inside the house during my night-time meanderings, it would be one thing, but I tend to wander. It's not just anyone who has ended up in her neighbor's kitchen making eggs Benedict at 3:00 a.m. or has been awakened by a policeman while in the 7-Eleven buying Tootsie Rolls and trying to pay for them with bus tokens.

My own home is wired with alarms so that if I open a door they wake not only me but the dead in three counties. Other places…well, that's a different matter.

"I'll let the front desk know," I assured Mickey. "If they see me leaving, they can bring me back."

"I don't know why you want this job anyway. It involves travel." Mickey's lips turned downward at the corners. "Your family is here. We'll take care of you."

True, they would take care of me, but they also have a lot of laughs at my expense. There's that running joke my brother, Mike, started when we were in high school that's only grown over the years. "How can you tell if Suze has been sleepwalking?" he would ask at the dinner table. "All the eggs in the carton are already fried!"

"…the washing machine is full of freshly washed shoes…."

"…the dog is wearing an undershirt and a pair of boxers…."

Fortunately Mike moved to Germany where he is teaching English and I have a two-year reprieve from his teasing.

I'm creative in my sleep. What's so bad about that?

Everything.

"I've never dared travel alone and it's time I

quit allowing my fear to rule me and to master this thing. I want to take care of myself and I want to travel."

"When you're sleepwalking no one realizes it, Suze. You talk and act like you are totally awake. What if you get mixed up with some horrible man or walk onto the freeway?"

"I'll buy another padlock. I am going, Mickey, and I don't want you to worry about me. I'll be fine." I didn't tell her I'd also considered buying a box of tacks to strew across the hotel-room floor, hoping that pain and blood would wake me up before I escaped.

"Okay, if you say so." She stood up and kissed me on the cheek. "Now I think I'll take the boys home and give you a break. You'll have plenty of them soon enough."

As I closed the door behind my sister and nephews, I leaned against it and sighed. Mickey was worried about my health and welfare, certainly. Didn't she realize that I'd probably be in more danger from the Terrors than wandering alone and asleep on Michigan Avenue?

Chapter Two

The flight from Minneapolis to Chicago took just over an hour, and I reached my hotel with plenty of time to check in and unpack before dinner. My college room-mate, Darla, is in middle management in the insurance company for which we work. She works in the Chicago office and picked me up at seven for dinner.

She held out her hands, wrapped her arms around me and squeezed tightly, like a hungry boa constrictor. "I have missed you so much. You never get to the Windy City to see me." She glanced at me sympathetically, dyed blond curls falling into her face. She scraped the hair from her eyes with her fingers. "I understand, of course, but I do wish you'd travel more. Come on, the car's this way."

I quickly got into her car.

"Are you nervous?" she asked. "About your interview?"

"It will be more money and a promotion but I have mixed feelings about the added travel."

She held up her hands and waggled her fingers as if to indicate something eerie. "Because of the woo-woo sleepwalking?"

Darla and I roomed together in college so she, more than most, knows the scope and gravity of my affliction.

"Remember the night we found you sitting on the front steps of the administration building trying to convince one of the stone lions to let you pet him? Or the time you took a shower in your pajamas?"

"I wasn't exactly awake to remember, Darla, but I've certainly heard about it enough. We graduated from college a while ago. Surely something interesting has happened since then that would be more fun to discuss."

Darla screwed up her face as if she were considering my statement. "Nope, I don't think so. Suze Charles sleepwalking stories are urban myths on campus by now. Have you forgotten the time you got into the cafeteria and set every table? Three hundred plates, cups and sets of silverware. You folded the paper napkins into little hats and everything."

"I've tried to forget, but no one will let me."

Of all the things I could be remembered for—my work with animal rescue, my graduation summa cum laude, my master's degree, the volunteer mission work for my church or even my ability to cross my eyes—but no, I'm famous for what I *don't* remember doing, all the mayhem I've caused in my sleep.

"At least you aren't a sleep eater. You don't raid the refrigerator at night," Darla said. "That, at least, is something to be grateful for."

"If I were, I'd be sunk—and weigh about three hundred pounds."

"But you're a sleep cooker and an amazing one, at that. You make better brownies sound asleep than I do wide awake. Remember the time you visited me over break and made fifteen pie crusts and left them rolled out all over the counters? Mom still tells stories about that."

Of course she does. Everyone who knows me tells stories about me. I'm the only one not conscious to enjoy them. A wave of despondency crashed over me. "Instead of outgrowing the sleepwalking, I'm afraid it's getting worse."

"If you ever decide to marry, your poor husband is going to be in for a lot of sleepless nights following you around, keeping you out of trouble." Darla is far too cheerful about this.

"Don't think I haven't considered it. I doubt any marriage could outlast the honeymoon with a bride like me. It's not romantic having to sleep with one's eyes open to make sure his new wife doesn't drown herself having a midnight dip in the motel swimming pool."

"Can you do something about it, Suze?"

How many times have I explained this to people over the years? Now I just try to avoid the subject entirely, if possible. "I've done everything I know how to do," I said, feeling flooded with resignation and no little amount of despair. "I drink decaffeinated beverages. I moved my television out of my bedroom. I exercise daily and I don't eat heavily before bedtime.

"Medications haven't helped. So far the ones I've taken have only slowed me down. My sister, Mickey, tells me I look like I'm sleep-walking underwater."

"There must be something more."

"My doctor said to try not to worry about things near bedtime. Of course, the one thing I really have to worry about *is* bedtime."

The only thing I've found that helps is Psalm 4:8. *In peace I will both lie down and sleep; for thou alone, O Lord, makes me dwell in safety.*

He is the only one I can count on to keep me safe both day and night. And I have to put my trust in Him every single time I close my eyes.

"Do you recall the time you…"

I was grateful when we pulled up at the restaurant and handed the car over to valet parking. As with anyone I know well, I have to endure at least twenty minutes of "remember whens" before I can have a sensible conversation with them. Even my sister is guilty of this. It's difficult to be so fascinating and unique that people can't quit talking about you.

Only my mother will cease and desist from the stories—and she's the one who once plucked me out of the bathtub fully clothed. She also found me standing between two halves of a bedspread draped over an outdoor clothesline at 2:00 a.m. I'm not sure what I thought I was doing there but apparently my feet were cold and damp and I was perfectly happy to crawl back into bed. I recalled nothing the next morning. After that, they put a little string attached to a bell across my bedroom door, hoping they'd hear me before I went for a nighttime walkabout. It was weeks before they realized that I was ducking under the string and escaping anyway.

As we entered the small and elegant café, a shiver of pleasure bled through me. Not that

Minneapolis doesn't have wonderful restaurants, but the idea of seeing something new—something in a city that required an overnight stay—is a thrill for me.

The hardwood floor was covered with durable Plexiglas. Threaded between the wood and the Plexiglas were thin tubes of pink neon lighting. The theme was echoed as zigzags of neon tubes shot around the room. Dark cherrywood and glass made the place look both elegant and contemporary. High-hatted chefs were working in the open kitchen.

"This is *the* new place to come," Darla informed me. "Anybody who is anyone can be found here."

"What about us? Who are we?"

She grinned at me. "We're just lucky enough to work for a company that woos all its potential employees here."

"I'm hardly 'potential.' I already work for them."

"True, but they really want you to take this job promotion. You have a great reputation and top brass is pleased that you finally have agreed to consider moving up the ranks."

After we were seated at a table near the center of the room, Darla studied me. "It's always been about fear, hasn't it?"

Her bluntness stung. Especially since it was true.

"Fear? I don't know if I'd use that strong a word. Okay, maybe I *would* use it. What if I make a spectacle of myself somewhere, wandering around in the night? Or got run over by a taxi cab? Or a horse and buggy in Central Park?"

Darla put her hand on my arm. "It's time to start living, Suze. You've been vigilant and careful all your life. I'm sure it was hard to be the late-night entertainment at junior-high slumber parties but now it is time to throw caution to the winds."

"Easy for you to say. You aren't the one who makes a fool of herself."

"What's a little foolishness if it frees you to live?"

Have my midnight meanderings kept me from living? In some ways yes, in others, no. I have a great education, a wonderful job at which I'm well respected, dozens of friends, a great family, the animals. I play softball in the summer and ski in the winter. I'm invited to lots of parties and am never at a loss for something to do. My home is cozy and welcoming and I'm a great cook. That doesn't sound like someone who is not living.

Of course, I rarely travel unless someone is

with me. I've almost reconciled myself to being a lonely spinster because I can't imagine any man signing up to watch over me for the rest of his life. And that's come to mind a lot more lately. Maybe I could meet someone like a prison guard or traffic cop, someone with sharp eyes who is accustomed to keeping people in line.

Perhaps Darla's right. Maybe I should be trusting God more and my elaborate alarm system less. I'm tired of being an almost thirty-year-old captive to my dreams and nighttime wanderings.

"Ooohhh," Darla squealed, sounding just as she had in college. "Hunk to the right, entering main door. Is that guy gorgeous or what? Is he wearing Armani?"

Darla entertains me with her constant man-watch. She's primed and ready to be married but is currently between significant others. Me? I haven't tried to find Mr. Right. What if, once I find him, he hears about my Dr. Jekyll and Mr. Hyde nighttime personalites, and he thinks I'm too complicated to bother with and runs?

It's happened before. It turned out to be a bigger nightmare than any I've had since. During my senior year of college I believed I was in love with the man of my dreams, a guy named Brandon. Brandon liked to be called "Brand" for short. That alone should have been warning sign enough, but I was so infatuated that I would have called him Mick Jagger if he'd asked. Looking back, I realize that Brand used my sleep issues, which took on mythical proportions around campus, to get out of his commitment to me. A raging commitment-phobe, Brand wasn't going to commit to an engagement with me or anyone. He simply used my weird nocturnal behavior as his excuse. What made me think we'd last as a couple anyway? Naive wishful thinking, that's what. It is all clear to me now, but I still remember how his lack of fidelity had hurt.

It's better not to put myself in another situation that could break my heart.

What husband wants his wife pouring ice water on his head during the night or calling the fire department to report a nonexistent fire? My own *father* once threatened to send me off to a boarding school with bars on the windows when I painted the fenders on his new Buick. If my own father couldn't stand it, how could a man whose blood didn't run in my veins?

She kicked me in the ankle. "Look, Suze! You can't miss this bit of scenery."

Reluctantly I turned my head. In the doorway stood a man about six foot two, with dark straight hair, brown eyes and a tanned complexion that made him look as if he'd just come from the beach. His features were even; his jaw firm and everything about him whispered elegance and sophistication. His suit cost more than my monthly mortgage. And his shoes? Well, they were worth at least a car payment.

Then he laughed at something his companion said and I saw a flash of white, even teeth.

"Worth turning your head for, don't you think?" Darla said slyly. "Who and what do you think he is? A movie star? A CEO? An ambassador?"

It was a game we'd played for years.

"King of a small country?" I offered.

"Too stuffy. Maybe he's a U.S. senator."

"Now *that's* too stuffy. I think he's a famous heart surgeon. Transplants. Saves lives."

"Or maybe a brain surgeon. I can just imagine him holding my little brain in the palms of his hands." Darla looked as though she were ready to drool.

Fortunately our desserts arrived at the moment and, entranced as she was with Mr. Gorgeous, she likes baked Alaska even more.

We lazed over our decaffeinated coffee until I glanced at my watch. "Darla, it is ten o'clock!

I've got to get some sleep or I'll blow my interview tomorrow."

"No chance. It's a formality."

I bent to pick up my purse from the floor and out of the corner of my eye saw the handsome object of our little game. He smiled and I felt as if he'd looked straight at me. I bumped my head on the underside of the table as I sat up, rattling the glassware. His smile grew as he turned away. That was smooth. Now I'm making a fool of myself while I'm awake, too. Fortunately I'd never see the man again.

Darla dropped me off at my hotel with instructions for tomorrow and an invitation to take me out to lunch when the interview was over. Back in my room at the hotel, I followed my evening ritual.

I ordered warm milk from room service, soaked in a soothing bath, lit a small candle called "Restful," which is tinged with essential oils meant to make me sleep, and sank into my softest cotton pajamas, ones covered with fluffy clouds and cute little sheep jumping over fences. Then I rigged my door with a little silver bell and propped a chair under the door handle. Unfortunately, no matter how hard I tried I couldn't figure out how to use my new padlock so I tossed it back into my suitcase, zippered the case shut and put that in front of the door as well. By the time I was done I'd constructed a barricade in my room much like the one I imagine Davy Crockett built at the Alamo.

Satisfied, I crawled into bed, fluffed the pillow I'd brought from home and opened my Bible.

There'd be no wandering tonight, I assured myself and dozed into a contented, even confident, sleep.

Chapter Three

I felt pulled up from a groggy fog, my head swimming and my legs heavy, and stared in horror at the clock on the bedside table— 8:00 a.m.! I must have dozed off again after I'd dressed for my interview and now, instead of being early, I would be lucky to be only minutes late. Not a good start.

I scrambled up, grabbed my purse and briefcase and went to the door where I was met with the obstacle course I'd built for myself the night before. With strength born of a job loss looming in my future, I hurled aside the suitcase, the chair, the garbage can and whatever else I'd managed to stack into the heap in front of the door. If I lost this job because I'd managed to blockade myself into my hotel room and couldn't get out...

The clatter I made should have awoken the dead, to say nothing of the people in the rooms on either side of or across from me, but perhaps they, unlike me, were already at their appointments.

I flung open the door and hesitated, confused. The hotel was cleverly built to resemble honeycombs. Just what I needed right now, a labyrinth to navigate. Willing myself not to scream in frustration, I walked to the left in an attempt to retrace my steps of the evening before. Where was an early-morning maid when I really needed one? If I'd *wanted* to sleep in today, at least three would have knocked on my door by now, singing out "maid service." But when I absolutely had to be up, the place was as silent as a tomb. The only sound was a spill of fresh ice tumbling somewhere inside the ice machine down the hall.

Ice machine. That was it. I remembered it being not far from the elevators. I headed toward the low grumble of the machine.

I moved quickly, my heart thumping hard, my briefcase clutched to my chest. If I couldn't make it to headquarters on time, how would they ever trust me to get to important appointments or meet significant clients? Seeing the job promotion slipping away into the ether, I finally found the ice machine. I was so nervous that my mouth felt like sawdust. There wouldn't be time to stop at a coffee cart for something to drink, so impulsively I plunged my hand into the ice bin, plucked out some cubes and popped one into my mouth. At least now my tongue would not stick to the roof of my mouth as I met the CEO of my company.

Now where was that elevator again?

I turned and ran full force into a wall.

A warm, not unpleasantly hard wall, but a wall, nonetheless. I pushed at it but it wouldn't move. I tried to step around it and it stepped with me. I attempted to shoulder it out of my way with no success. Finally, I made a fist and tried to punch my way past and elicited a small "Uh" from it. As I drew my elbow back and curled my hand into a tighter fist, the wall grabbed my wrist. No matter how hard I wrestled, its grip was implacable. Trapped! Just like something out of an Edgar Allan Poe story! No matter which way I moved, the wall was in front of me.

Terrified, I did the only thing I knew to do— I started to scream.

Suddenly a hand clapped over my mouth, and I felt myself being propelled along the hallway so quickly that my feet barely touched the ground. I was being kidnapped! Immediately my mind went to some of the terrible things that would no doubt happen to me. My poor parents. They'd probably never know what became of me. And Darla! She would feel so responsible. What would my company think? They'd flown me here to offer me a significantly higher job position. Would they believe I'd run off? My reputation would be ruined. Of course, what's a good reputation if I'm spirited away and kept prisoner in some madman's basement?

Right where I was, I dropped to my knees and prayed.

Help me! You are the only one who can get me out of this! Let the elevator door open and a janitor or a maid find us. You are my protector. Spread protection over me that, like David, I may rejoice in You....

And that was where I was when I began to wake up, on my knees in one of the small meeting rooms the hotel provided, praying out loud as the incredibly handsome man I'd seen in the restaurant last night sat in the chair across from me, a cup of coffee in one hand, calmly watching me as if he dealt with frantic, maniacal sleepwalkers every day.

My hands were wet from the now-melted ice

cubes and I realized that I was not dressed for the day in my business suit at all but still in my sheep-and-cloud pajamas. What I'd thought was my briefcase was actually my makeup kit. I'd squeezed it so hard that the cap had come off my toothpaste and was oozing out the top like mint-green glue. The clock on the wall said 3:00 a.m.

Well, God had protected me, all right. He'd protected me from running into the street and being hit by a cab. He had not protected me, however, from profound humiliation and intense mortification the likes of which—even in all my years of sleepwalking and waking in odd situations—I'd never before experienced.

Instead of looking shocked or horrified, however, the gentleman, whose white shirt, even at 3:00 a.m., was completely unwrinkled and crisp, looked mildly interested and not the least surprised by the raving mess he'd found eating cubes out of the hotel ice machine.

"Are you waking up?" he inquired calmly, gently.

I groaned and rocked forward on my knees to bury my face in my hands. All I wanted to do was to disappear into the carpet. "Yes. Just check me into an institution now. If it walks like a duck and it quacks like a duck, it must be a duck. If it walks like a psycho and yammers like a psycho, it must be a psycho. I am so embarrassed that I want to die."

"No need for that. I understand." He stood up and offered me his hands. I scrambled to my feet and was momentarily glad that my flannel jammies were the least revealing items in my entire wardrobe. I stumbled close to him as I rose and caught a whiff of some spicy cologne.

His eyes, dark and astute, were also kind. I felt compassion from his every pore. Usually people are either horror-struck or amused by my sleep antics. Both amazed and startled by his unusual response, I allowed him to lead me to a sofa and settle me in one corner. He pulled up a chair and sat across from me.

If possible, he was even better looking up close. Firm jawline, intelligent eyes, finely shaped mouth, a high forehead over which dark hair feathered. Then he smiled and I thought my heart might leap out of my body through my throat. He was not the kind of man I—or any woman—would choose as a witness to her embarrassment.

Too late. I should have crawled under the rug when I was down on my knees.

"I am so sorry," I stammered. "I'm sure you think I'm certifiable and should be locked up immediately, but I'm not, really. It's just that I…"

"Suffer from parasomnia? You obviously have a REM sleep disorder of some sort. Probably several other things going on as well—somnambulism, periodic limb movement, other arousal disorders. Night terrors, perhaps. Sleepwalking is nothing to be ashamed of. Granted, it's embarrassing, but hardly within your control."

"You know about…me?" Relief sprang within me; someone understood. I was also hopeful. I had not sent this Adonis of a man off screaming for help and demanding the demented woman wandering the hallways be hauled away.

"Not you in particular, but I recognize your behavior. Many people with parasomnias have nocturnal dramas such as yours—or much worse."

"Worse?"

"Oh, yes. I've been involved in more than one court case explaining how perfectly sane and rational people can exhibit aggressive dream enactments. Murders, even."

"Who are you anyway?" I was beginning to feel I'd awoken from one dream only to find myself in another.

"I'm sorry I didn't introduce myself." He smiled at me in a way that activated every nerve fiber in my body. "Dr. David Grant. I'm a neurologist and administrator of a new institute for brain research and sleep disorders in Minneapolis."

Institute, institution. Brain disorders. The perfect guy for me.

"Do you always wander the halls of hotels at 3:00 a.m. rescuing sleepwalkers?"

He laughed. It was an agreeable rumble deep in his chest. When he smiled, his expression dissolved into pleasant lines around his eyes. "Purely accidental. I've been overseas and my inner time clock isn't working properly. After the restaurant closed I found an all-night coffee shop. I'm a people watcher so it was good entertainment."

"The restaurant..." I mumbled.

"Yes. I noticed you there with your friend."

"You did?" I hoped he hadn't overheard us behaving like silly schoolgirls. Wait until I tell Darla I met this man of our dreams! And that I met him in my sheep-and-clouds pajamas... eating ice out of a machine... clutching my makeup kit...falling on my knees to pray....

Coming to my senses I vowed that I would never, *ever* tell this to Darla or any other living soul. No matter how much fun my friends would have at my expense, I would take this Suze the Sleepwalker story to my grave.

Chapter Four

Now what? How does one squirm one's way out of a situation this awkward? I felt as low as a worm so I should have been able to wiggle like one.

"I suppose I'd better get back to my room, although I know I will never be able to fall asleep again. My heart is pounding like a trip hammer. It happens sometimes when I finally wake up and realize where I am or what I've been doing."

"I don't expect to sleep either, not for a few hours, at least. Would you like to get something to eat?"

That shocked me almost as much as waking up at his feet yelling out prayers to God. "Me? Eat?" I said inanely.

"You do get hungry, don't you?" There was

a twinkle of humor in his coffee-colored eyes now. I realized that, although he had not thought my sleepwalking was funny, he was now amused by my wakefulness.

"Of course I do, but look at me. I'm wearing ridiculous pajamas and have squeezed toothpaste all over myself. I'm hardly ready to be seen in public."

"Change, I'll wait. I have all night."

Why, I'm not sure, other than his compelling expression and the encouraging twitch of a smile on his face, but I got up and did his bidding.

I crawled over the stack of furniture, suitcases and detritus I'd left at the door to my room, ditched the pajamas and slipped into the pair of jeans and sweater I'd planned to wear tomorrow on the plane ride home. Hardly glamorous. Barely attractive, even. For the first time I realized that I seem to have critters of various breeds on all my clothing. The sweater was an old Ralph Lauren with the head of a horse knit right over my chest. Sheep, horses, what was next? Aardvarks?

Dr. Grant was still waiting for me in the small meeting room when I returned. He was reading a business magazine and when he looked up, he smiled. Oh, brother, did he smile. The boyish smile indicated a playfully charming side of Dr. Grant that his polished, sophisticated exterior did not. My heart started to pound again. Just what I *didn't* need right now. An attraction attack. Handsome as this man was, he would never see me again after tonight. I'd already promised myself to make sure of it.

"Ready?" He stood from his chair like an athlete and I knew that beneath his tailored suit was a superb body, sinewy and strong.

Well, slap your own face, Suze! I had no business thinking about things like *that*.

"I suppose so, even though I have no idea where we'll find an open restaurant at this time of night."

"Not far from here, actually. I've flown into Chicago from Europe before. After a few sleepless nights in the city, one discovers these things."

We went down the elevator together and other than an odd look from the man at the desk and a sleepy doorman, we escaped unnoticed. It was clear that I couldn't depend on even a doorman to keep me in the hotel if necessary.

"It's just over a block from here. Do you mind walking?"

"You mean that if I did that you would call a cab to take us?" Now that is a gentleman.

"Of course."

"Nonsense. It's a warm night. Let's go."

The diner was a hole-in-the-wall affair but surprisingly busy. Apparently there were more night owls out and about than I had realized. One man sat on a stool and swayed to the music from his iPod that only he could hear. A homeless man was curled up in a booth nursing a cup of coffee. A table full of male college students was laughing and talking.

"Hey, Dr. Dave, back again?" a man in a greasy apron greeted us. "And a pretty lady with you this time."

"What have you got that's good this time of night?""

"The pancakes are always good." The man gave us a grin in which every other tooth seemed to be missing. "And I already started the soup for today. And making bread."

The charming doctor looked at me inquiringly.

"Pancakes," I murmured. "Early breakfast."

"Very early." Toothless said, "I'll bring you some bacon with that. Doc?"

"I'll have the same. And a couple eggs, easy over, please."

"Gotcha."

"And the same for my friend over there." The doctor pointed to the homeless man in the booth.

"Nice of you. I was going to have to kick him out soon if he didn't order something to eat." Our waiter-chef-business owner turned away. He was wearing a white T-shirt that had shrunk in the wash and a pair of low-riding trousers with that plumber-under-the-sink sort of look.

I wondered wildly what I'd gotten myself into now.

Good food, I realized, when he returned some moments later with stacks of high, fluffy pancakes topped with real butter and a pitcher of warm maple syrup. He set a large plate of eggs and bacon on the table between us and two side orders of sausage.

"Thank you but I didn't order eggs...."

He skewered me with an appraising glance.

"Too skinny. Eat 'em. I like women with meat on their bones." He turned to my dining companion. "How about you, Doc?"

Now the two men were eyeing me.

"I always respect the personal taste of others," the doctor said, obliquely. "And the food looks great."

The other man didn't even know he'd been dismissed.

"You're providing me with a very...special... experience, Dr. Grant. The food looks wonderful."

"Please, call me David." He pushed the maple syrup my way. "Let's eat first while the food is still warm. We'll talk later."

I had no argument with him about the food. It was like ambrosia to my taste buds and to my own amazement, I cleaned my plate.

Settling back with a cup of steaming coffee, Doctor…David, renewed his study of my face. "Want to tell me about it?"

"About what?" Of course I knew what he was talking about but played dumb anyway. Talking about my weird sleeping habits didn't make them go away.

"How long has this been a problem for you?"

I sighed. He wasn't going to give up without an answer. "Forever, I think. My mother and father talk about finding me roaming around the house and talking in my sleep ever since I was a child. In fifth or sixth grade, I went to a slumber party, fell asleep and I turned into the evening's entertainment. I told everyone about all the boys I liked, why I liked them and which of them I planned to marry when I grew up. I also, with encouragement, got up and filled my own underwear with water and put it in the freezer. I nearly froze to death on my way home the next morning.

"Some snitch, Mary Ellen Jenkins, I think,

told everyone she knew. I practically had to wear a paper bag over my head for the rest of the year. I couldn't look anyone in the eye—especially not the boys."

I stirred cream into my coffee and made a note to come back to this place every time I was in Chicago. The atmosphere was iffy but the food definitely made up for it. "Things went downhill from there. School trips, overnights as a cheerleader when the team traveled, summer camp, sleepovers, all a disaster. No one ever knew what I was going to do, least of all me." I looked up at him, trying to smile. "Let's just say it made me into a bit of a homebody. I didn't sleep away from home much until I went to college. Thankfully I met my friend Darla there. She was a gift from God. Even though I made a fool of myself plenty of times, who knows how many disasters she diverted?"

Unexpectedly, tears came to my eyes. I wiped them away furiously, hating the vulnerability and frustration I felt. "I'm used to it by now."

"I see that," David murmured, "by the way it doesn't affect you."

He'd seen right through me.

"You don't have to be cynical about it. It's just tears. It's not like my life is a big mess or anything."

"You don't have to prove anything to me, Miss…"

"Suze, call me Suze."

"Suze. I've seen hundreds of patients with your disorder, and it can make chaos of people's lives."

"Well, I haven't murdered anyone if that's what you mean. I've just come to accept the fact that this is the way I am and there's nothing that can be done about it."

"Are you sure about that?"

"Yes, I am. There's no way I'm holding out hope any longer. I've had my hopes up too many times and every time they have been dashed. Medications have failed, routines have been futile. There is nothing left to be done for me."

I'd put my faith in several doctors, all of whom had disappointed me.

"I can't say for sure, but I beg to differ."

"Your other clients haven't been me," I pointed out. "Unless you have a team of brilliant scientists eager to solve an unanswerable question and the ability to work scientific miracles, I'm never going to change." That is something I believe with my whole heart. I had a lifetime of tests, doctors and unhelpful advice to back up my theory.

"Actually, I do, have brilliant scientists, I mean. I told you that I'm administrator for an institute that studies problems such as yours. I've got a very bright team who would be more than happy to take a look at you."

"Study the newest monkey in the cage?" I wasn't sure why I was being so stubborn about this whole thing—deathly embarrassment, I suppose, but I couldn't stop myself.

"If that's how you think of it. I'm not taking patients right now, but I do have a physician who is as good as any I've ever met. I could get you in to see him if you'd like."

A flicker of hope sparked within me but was immediately doused by all the failures I'd experienced in the past.

"Thank you, but I'm not interested in having more electrodes attached to my head." Impulsively I laid my hand on his arm as it rested on the table. "But I appreciate the offer. You've been more than kind. I really don't know how to apologize for how I behaved earlier."

"Would you apologize for being diabetic?"

"Of course not…"

"Then don't apologize for this. It's a condition, Suze, not a crime. And it doesn't have to be a prison for life. I think we could help you."

"I've heard it before," I assured him. "Thanks, but no thanks."

Even though he quietly laid his business card on the table and pushed it toward my hand, David was gracious enough to accept my rebuff and we finished our coffee chatting about safer things—the weather, the Minnesota Twins and road construction around the city—nothing that even hinted at nighttime meanderings.

Chapter Five

Dr. Grant was nowhere to be seen when I left the hotel for my interview. I was thankful and yet a bit disappointed. I didn't want his institute playing with my mind but on a personal level I had enjoyed our 3:00 a.m. breakfast very much.

It was as if I'd dreamed of him the night before and none of it had actually happened. In my condition that could be true. Maybe I *had* dreamed up the dazzling Dr. David Grant.

Darla pulled up at the hotel's front door as I stood outside watching for her. She waved me into the car and peered at me, her big blue eyes round and questioning. "Are you nervous?"

"Not particularly." I buckled my seat belt.

This is nothing compared to what happened a few hours ago, I mused silently. A piece of cake. There's no way I can disgrace myself any more than I had in the middle of the night.

"Good, because you are a shoo-in. It's my guess that they're already thinking about your travel schedule. They'll start you out easy, I know, but they're excited to have someone with your experience onboard."

Travel. My favorite thing, right up there with having toenails removed and black widow spiders.

"You know, maybe I shouldn't interview for this job," I said tentatively. "It's not very practical for someone like me…."

"Someone like you? You're exactly who they need."

"What *I* may need is a keeper, have you thought of that? I'll have to hire someone to travel with me and make sure I stay in my room at night."

"Can't you do something?" Darla's brow furrowed. "*Anything?* Maybe doctors have discovered something new since you went through that routine before."

I'm generally an optimistic person but I felt a wave of hopelessness crash over me. My sleep habits were the one thing that could bring me down off my usually happy and contented high.

"I've tried it all, Darla. Frankly, I've accepted the fact that this is my affliction, my cross to bear." That sounded overly dramatic and theatrical to even my ears but it's how I feel sometimes. "Maybe I'm a fool for even considering…"

"Stop it." Her voice was harsh with frustration. Then she took my hand as we paused at a stoplight. I felt concern and affection pouring from her. "I've been praying about this for a long time, Suze. God will answer. He always does."

"Sometimes He says, 'No.'"

"And sometimes He says, 'Wait, I have something better planned.' It isn't like you to be so despondent."

"Hey." I felt my smile waver tremulously. "I'll snap out of it. I always do."

"Well, start snapping. Here we are. You've got to have your head together for this interview."

I've always loved Chicago—the lake, the pier, the cruise boats that sail at night, allowing passengers to look back at the lovely skyline decorated with high-rise buildings and twinkling lights. In Chicago, I even enjoy the wind. Nowhere else, however, just in Chicago. And the shopping! I could rhapsodize about it for hours.

Darla pulled up in front of an imposing

building and I felt my stomach take a roller-coaster ride into the soles of my shoes.

No need to be nervous, I told myself. I've been to the main office of my insurance company a dozen times on day trips, flying in and out on the same day for meetings.

But this time was different and I knew it. I was attempting to do something I hadn't done before—intentionally turn my life on its ear. The traveling that came with this job, if I got it, was a challenge I'd finally have to face, a mountain I'd have to climb. There was something inside me desperately wanting to push myself out of the comfortable nest I'd created and to tackle the one thing that kept my life from being nearly perfect.

Maybe it was the specter of never traveling by myself for fear of what I might get into. Or perhaps it was the fact that I was going to be Terry and Tommy's spinster aunt, the funny one who is set in her ways and always wears her clothing and hair as if she were trapped in another decade. Odd Auntie Suze. Sweet, pleasant, fearful.

I could imagine Mickey whispering to the boys and their wives someday, "She should have married and had children but you know about her PROBLEM...." The way Mickey would say *problem* it would no doubt sound as if it were written in capital letters. "She never thought any man would want to marry a woman who was so unpredictable in her sleep. A shame, really. Did I ever tell you about the time she actually drove her car to an all-night restaurant in St. Paul and asked for Belgian waffles to go?"

Although I didn't admit it to Mickey or anyone else, it's not far off—me giving up, that is, and permanently having to reconcile myself to the fact that my sleep activities were keeping me from ever living a normal life.

So here I am, riding the elevator to the thirty-fifth floor to interview for a job that will throw everything I fear my way. It's like jumping off the high dive and then checking to see if there's water in the pool, but what else can I do?

"Suze! Welcome!" Clifford Ford, owner and president of Restwell Insurers Mutual, greeted me. *Restwell Insurers*. Ironic, isn't it, that a company that guarantees its customers that they will sleep better at night with all their insurance needs met would have me as an employee?

"Hello, Mr. Ford, nice to see you again."

I was immediately disappointed when he said, "I am double-booked today so I'm unable to sit in on your interview. Everyone is looking forward to seeing you. Now if you'll come this way…"

I had an inkling of what it must have been like for the sad souls who made their last trip over the Rio di Palazzo, on the Bridge of Sighs in Venice. The bridge connects the Doge's Palace with the prisons and it's said that the view from the bridge was the last thing convicts saw on their way to prison.

I'd never been so confused. This whole interview and potential job are a classic approach-avoidance conflict in a nutshell. And I'm the nut. If I get it I'll be terrified; if I don't get it I'll be devastated. Fear or rejection. Trepidation or rebuff—which to choose? Neither. But that's not an option. One or the other is going to be the new theme of my life.

Restwell Insurers Mutual does everything tastefully, even interviews. The relaxed atmosphere of the interview room, its comfy chairs and good pastries lulled me into complacency. I felt so at home, in fact, that I was not as cautious as I might have been. They caught me a time or two doing my best deer-in-the-headlights imitation.

"Tell me, Ms. Charles, are you open to overseas travel? We've acquired a company in

London and plan to send some of our people to that office to train staff there."

I was struck with fish mouth—wide and gaping.

"There's been an upsurge in claims in the southeastern part of the country. Would you consider traveling for as long or two or three weeks at a time?" That question had me gasping for air like a guppy that had jumped out of the bowl and onto the carpet.

Two or three weeks? Ha! They had no idea how much trouble I could get into in just an hour or two.

Funny how a dream come true can also be a nightmare in the making.

Apparently my head was at least together enough to get me the job.

"Your interview must have been amazing," Darla gushed when I met her in the lobby on the first floor of the building.

"How would you know?"

She blushed to the roots of her artificially blond hair. "I was in the coffee room when two of the execs who interviewed you came in."

"Were you spying for me?"

"Not exactly. Choosing my placement carefully, maybe. Making sure I was within earshot?

Perhaps. Spying? That's too James Bond-ish for me." She twinkled at me with her baby blues. It is completely impossible to stay annoyed with Darla. "They were raving about you."

"As in stark raving mad?"

Though Darla chortled, I, recalling myself break out of my own room last night, could not laugh with her.

As I waited to board the plane back to Minneapolis–St. Paul, I watched important-looking businessmen stride back and forth carrying briefcases. None was better looking than the handsome Dr. Grant.

If wishing could make something so, I would wish that David Grant's clinic actually could help me, but after years of disappointment I'd already decided that I would have to handle my problem my way and learn to live with it.

The short plane trip home was uneventful, which was fortunate for the other passengers. Exhausted from the night before, I fell asleep before we were airborne and, strapped in as I was, stayed right where I was supposed to be.

Mickey was waiting for me outside baggage claim. I tossed my suitcase into the back of her car and hopped in the front with her.

"What? No boys?"

"They're at Mom's. I couldn't take it any-

more. I'm trying to pack and also to get everything ready for when we return with the baby.
Every time I turned my back they'd undo something I've just done." She looked at me with
worried eyes. "Are you sure they won't be too
much for you, Suze?"

"I go to the gym every evening. I take
vitamins, avoid white sugar and flour. I juice
my own fruits and veggies. If I'm not fit to take
them on, who is?"

Mickey's shoulders slumped. "Mom says
she'll help all she can, but I know she and Dad
would have a meltdown if they had to keep
track of the boys for three months."

Most mortals would.

I smiled encouragingly at my sister. "We'll
be fine. Come back with that baby sister and
any problems we might have will disappear
like smoke."

Smoke. I made a mental note to remove all
matches from my house.

"In fact, why don't we do a trial run
tonight?" I suggested. "Tommy and Terry can
stay with me so you can finish getting ready.
You and Jeff could use a few hours together
without their 'help.' Bring them over just before
bedtime."

Mickey looked at me with pathetic gratitude

in her eyes. "You're the best sister in the entire world, Suze. I really appreciate it. But don't you have a date tonight or something?"

"Nope, not tonight." Although Mickey didn't know it, I've taken myself out of the dating circuit for a few months. I'm almost afraid to fall in love and don't want to take the chance.

Dr. Grant had said it himself: people can do anything in their sleep including commit murder. What if I married and the first time my husband and I had a fight I pasted him to the sheets with superglue or shredded all his suits with a toenail clipper? I know it's my discouragement speaking but better safe than sorry.

The boys arrived at 7:00 p.m. smelling like soap, shampoo and watermelon with a whiff of licorice thrown in. They were in their pajamas and Jeff carried one boy in each arm. They lay sleepily against their daddy's shoulders, each sucking a thumb. How could anything so cute be so destructive? Maybe they were changing. They were getting older and would be five on their next birthday. Maturity had to set in eventually.

"They're about ready to conk out," Jeff informed me. "And they will sleep all night without moving. Since they gave up naps, they run themselves ragged by evening. It's the saving grace for Mickey and me."

That and the fact that the boys had abandoned their habit of speaking in what I call "twin talk." They'd developed their own personal language about the time they'd learned to talk and had communicated with each other in what sounded to us like babble. It was really alarming to know that they could be hatching plans to destroy us all right in front of us and we didn't have a clue.

We tucked the boys into my spare bed and they curled up and snuggled in like two sleepy kittens. Chipper, the three-footed dog, jumped onto the bed and burrowed in with them. They looked like a photo from a Hallmark card, the three of them clumped into a bundle of dog and boys. One of them was snoring lightly. Probably Chipper.

At the door, just before he left, my brother-in-law took me by the shoulders and looked deep into my eyes. Jeff and I have known each other for many years and he's one of my favorite people. He can also read me like a book.

"Listen, Suze, Mickey hasn't said anything and I'm not sure she's even noticed because she's been so frantic about this trip but I see it."

"See what?"

"You're down in the dumps."

"Is it so apparent?"

"This job opportunity is what you've wanted, isn't it?"

"Yes. Of course."

"And you're scared spitless of the travel."

"It's an approach-avoidance kind of thing." I didn't admit how upset I am about my bizarre night in Chicago. "I think I can manage it but it is worrisome."

"I've done everything you've asked, Suze. I put extra locks on the windows and doors, turned down the temperature on your water heater. You've told all the neighbors that you'll have the boys so they can watch out for you. I think we've taken enough precautions. You'll be great. And maybe, if you quit worrying about it, you'll sleep better."

"Maybe," I said without much optimism. "And thanks for caring."

"Listen, if the boys get to be too much, you can hire extra help…."

"Get out of here!" I pointed sternly toward his car. "Take your wife out to eat. Pack your bags. Now scram."

Jeff grinned at me, saluted and, after he had transferred two toddler booster seats to my vehicle, did as he was told.

I checked on the boys again, tried to watch an inane movie on television and finally decided to go to bed as well. I put on the silky pajamas Mickey had given me for my birthday, turned on some ocean sounds and lay down. I went to sleep repeating Psalm 3:5. *Lie down and sleep: I wake again for the Lord sustains me.*

Chapter Six

I swam upward from the bottom of a deep lake of sleep, drawn by an odd sound coming from the other bedroom. Someone was choking. Tommy… Terry…

I ran, barefoot, into the spare room where a croupy Terry was hacking and barking in his sleep like a baby seal. Mickey had described the sound to me last time the boys were sick but now I heard it for myself and it was terrifying. His breathing was heavy and labored. I put my hand on his forehead and it felt strangely warm. His hair was glued to his skin. I had to get Terry to a hospital.

I knew I should call Mickey and Jeff, but I didn't want to risk taking the time for them to get here, so I threw a raincoat over my pajamas, picked up the groggy boys and carried them to the car. They were light in my arms even though I felt Terry struggle. The hacking sound grew worse.

What if something happened to either of them on my watch? I'd never forgive myself. Never.

Grateful that Jeff had had the presence of mind to leave the toddler seats, I buckled them in, firmly pulling on the lap seat belt, opened the garage door and attempted to start the engine. My hands were shaking so hard that I couldn't get the key into the ignition. I laid my head on the wheel and attempted to slow my breathing.

Calm down. Just calm down. Just start the car. You are less than five minutes from the hospital. I talked myself out of my panic and I attempted to fit the key into the ignition. Shaking as I was, I could barely hold it in my hand.

Had I picked up the wrong key in my haste? I stared at the silver object. No, it was my key. I'd know it anywhere. Oddly, in the dimness of the garage it also looked a good deal like a teaspoon.

A *teaspoon?* I broke the surface of the water and woke up.

I was sitting in the front seat of my car all right, in my pajamas and a raincoat, trying to fit the narrow end of a teaspoon into my ignition. I shook my head foggily. Maybe I'd been asleep, but I knew I'd heard someone choking. I turned to the back seat of my car where the boys' car seats sat and felt a blush of heat run through my body, followed by a humiliated chill. There, in one of the toddler seats, was Chipper, growling and chewing at the restraints. He was fitted into the system of belts and buckles, his little rump in the seat, his hind legs sticking out stiffly through the openings where Tommy or Terry's legs would be. He was snarling frantically and gnawing at the black seat-belt straps that held him fast.

I reached over and popped the release. He scrambled out of the booster, dove for the floor of the car and wriggled himself beneath the front seat where he lay whimpering. I put my hands on the wheel and rested my forehead on them. No wonder I'd thought Terry's forehead had seemed matted with hair. I'd felt for the temperature of a *dog*.

It was likely that Chipper had been twitching and growling in his sleep, something he often did when he was dreaming.

Speaking of dreaming… My dreams are getting worse lately. I'm reverting back to the activity level of my youth. I have acted on them more often in recent months and my behavior was significantly more bizarre.

What if I'd tried to drive? Even if I didn't back right through my garage door, I still might have hit a fence or tree. Or maybe I would have felt the need to speed while I took my ill nephew to the hospital. Then I would have had to explain to some nice police officer why my beloved nephew seriously resembled a Pekingese.

Worse yet, what if I *had* put the boys and not Chipper into the car and had an accident? The thought chilled me. I could have hurt or killed them.

I felt my tears leak onto the tops of my hands as I listened to poor, innocent Chipper recover from his toddler car–seat trauma. I desperately want my sister to go to South America and bring home their new baby. I want to give her peace of mind that her boys are safe with someone who loves them as much as she does. And I can't do either as long as my nighttime escapades put myself or anyone else in jeopardy.

Lord, show me what to do! Should I tell Mickey I can't watch the boys? Should I hire a babysitter for me? Do You want me to resign from the new job? Why me, Lord? Why this?

When I'd eventually pulled myself together, I let Chipper run around in the backyard to

release some pent-up emotional energy. He
chugged around in those frantic doggy circles
that I call frenetic puppy activity. He reminded
me of a furry pressure cooker letting off steam.
Then I bribed my way back into his good
graces with bacon treats and carried him like a
king back to the twins' bed.

They were still asleep but each had somehow
managed to stick a thumb in the other's mouth.
Sucking each other's thumbs. A metaphor, I
realized, for the way these two function. Together
they are one terrifyingly bright mind replete with
uncontrolled impulses. They are inquisitive,
naughty, adorable and incorrigible. Suddenly the
time that Mickey and Jeff were going to be away
stretched before me like a vast wilderness of in-
hospitable territory and I had no roadmap.

Wearily, I spread a comforter on the floor in
front of the guest-room door and lay down on
it. This way the twins couldn't get up and
escape without having to wake me and the hard
floor would keep me from falling into a too
deep and unpredictable sleep.

I awoke to the sensation of having my eyelashes plucked out one by one.

A tiny thumb and index finger tugged at my
eyelid. The little fingers managed to open my
eye and Terry peered inquisitively at my blood-

shot eyeball. His hair was tousled and standing on end, his cheeks rosy and his breath warm against my cheek.

Then Tommy moved into view. They stared at me as if I were a most interesting find, almost as good as a frog, a grasshopper or even a garter snake.

"Good morning, boys." My voice sounded as though the frog had taken up residence in my throat during the night.

They looked at each other as if I'd said the most hilarious thing ever and fell on me giggling and tickling. Then Chipper jumped into the fray, locked his teeth around the leg of my pajamas and pulled, growling ferociously and wagging his tail. By the time I fought off the attack, pulled my pajamas back into place and crawled—literally—into the kitchen to get orange juice, I was ready to return to bed. Terry and Tommy, however, had other ideas.

They wanted to make breakfast.

My sister keeps the boys occupied by teaching them to "help" around the house. It's a pointless and naive exercise as far as I'm concerned but Mickey is a perennial optimist. Harebrained, loopy, impractical, you name it, that's Mickey where these boys are concerned.

While I forced my trembling hands to hold

a glass steady and pour juice into it, the twins managed to get a frying pan out of my lower cupboard and a carton of eggs from the refrigerator. From now on I must a) padlock my refrigerator and b) quit stocking my eggs on the lowest shelf.

By the time I'd captured those wonderful first dribbles of coffee from the pot in my mug, they'd cracked an entire dozen eggs into the pan as it sat on the kitchen floor.

If Mickey is going to teach those boys to cook, she has *got* to teach them that they must take the eggshells *out* of the pan, not drop them in on top of the eggs.

"Buckfest," Tommy said proudly as he pointed to the gelatinous and crunchy mess in my stainless-steel frying pan.

"I don't think you want to eat that for buckfest…er…breakfast, sweetie. How about some nice oatmeal with a banana?"

They looked at me as if I'd lost my mind.

"Your mother might buy you that sugar-coated, poisonous colored cereal that would give a boulder a sugar buzz, but at my house we eat healthy food."

Like warm milk, turkey and other foods containing tryptophan, to make you sleepy. Anything to take the edge off their energy.

They were happily eating oatmeal with bananas and raisins when the phone rang. It was Darla.

"Hi, have you received official confirmation of the job yet?"

"Not yet." I stepped into the living room so I didn't have to compete with Elmo on the kitchen television.

"Don't worry about it. You're in. You just haven't received the letter yet. Wait until I tell you the latest scuttlebutt. Someone from the Chicago office is going to be transferred to your office in Minneapolis. I'm hoping it will be me. Wouldn't that be fun?"

Darla loves a juicy bit of idle talk.

One thing I can say about my sister, Mickey, is that she is definitely not a gossip. If I tell her something, it goes nowhere else. She hasn't always been this way but ever since the twins were born, rumor, hearsay and chitchat have been low on her list.

Now I know why. Having a conversation with anyone, especially about something spicy that can divert one's full attention, is an exercise in self-sabotage. It distracts from the job at hand—keeping the twins out of mischief.

Suddenly I noticed a deafening silence coming from the kitchen. No Elmo, no boys, nothing.

"I have to go. I've got the boys...."

"Then why are you talking to me? I'm hanging up right now." Her receiver clicked in my ear.

The boys were no longer in the kitchen. Their cereal bowls were abandoned on the floor next to their chairs. Chipper was happily cleaning up the leftovers.

High-pitched giggles from my laundry room told me where the Terrors had gone. After a nasty experience Mickey had had with the boys, a bucket of water and fifteen bars of soap, I had began using up my toxic cleaning supplies and replacing them with all-natural laundry products. Only some powdered laundry soap was left and that was on a high shelf.

But when had high shelves ever stopped the Terrors before?

There aren't any shelves high enough to keep the world safe from the Terror Twins. They have the genetic makeup of spider monkeys— less-than-complex brains, acrobatic skills, swiftness and the ability to cover large areas by swinging arm over arm across large empty spaces. What makes it all worse is that they, unlike spider monkeys, are also gifted with opposable thumbs. Like the spider monkeys that rarely come down from the treetops in the rain-forest, the Terror Twins prefer to live in the rarified atmosphere over the tops of large pieces of furniture, refrigerators, tree houses and bunk beds.

Mickey and Jeff were forced to sell their lovely two-story home last year when they realized that they couldn't prevent the boys from plotting the best way to launch them-selves off the second-floor loft to see if they could fly. They now live in a staid rambler, which hasn't helped much. What they really should have done is move into a padded cell for a few years where no one could get hurt.

With a sense of foreboding, I peered into the laundry room.

It didn't look so bad at first, just detergent spread like snowflakes across the room. Tommy and Terry were systematically splash-ing water from Chipper's dog dish with tea-spoons onto the floor. Soap and water. They'd been into much worse things than that.

Of course, I had no idea that wet laundry powder dries to the hardness of concrete.

By the time Jeff arrived to pick up the children, it took everything in me not to drop to my knees and kiss his feet in gratitude.

As we stuffed the kids into their jackets like

sausage meats into casings, he gave me a worried look. "Are you sure you're going to be able to do this, Suze? They're quite a handful."

"It's not that. I just didn't get much sleep last night. We'll be fine."

He looked doubtful but didn't argue.

I stood in the door and waved as he carried the twins down my front walk. The boys waved sweetly at me and Tommy began sending air kisses my way.

So darling and so exhausting. I have to figure out how to get a good night's rest when I have the guys. Otherwise I'll never make it. I closed the door and sagged, my back against the firm wood. But how?

Chapter Seven

A human being can survive longer without food than she can without sleep. How long? It appears I'm going to find out.

If I board up the window in the twins' room, sleep on a cot inside the bedroom door and have my friend Charley come over and seal us in every night, then, perhaps I'd be assured that I and the twins would not have nighttime adventures not fit for children. But what if there were a fire? I'd also have to hire someone to sleep *outside* my door to sound the alarm and let us out. And if I'm going to do all this, I might as well hire someone else to watch the twins entirely.

The phone rang. It was Darla again. This time there was no chatty preamble. "Suze, remember the rumor about someone being transferred into your office from Chicago?

Well, it's *me!*" She did that high-pitched, for-dogs-only squeal at which preteen girls are so proficient. "Can you believe it? I'll get more pay and we can spend lots of time together."

My mouth was working as I tried to get a word in edgewise.

"I have to look for a place to live so I'm coming in tonight. Can I stay with you until I find something?"

"Of course you can."

She shrieked again. "It will be so fun!"

"Do you want me to pick you up at the airport?"

"I'll meet you outside baggage claim at six o'clock. Gotta go!" Abruptly she hung up and I was left staring at the receiver in my hand.

A wave of gratitude crashed over me and I grew limp with relief. Help would arrive. Darla was coming. She could lend a hand—or two—while I had the twins.

Although my family knows how I am, my sister and parents have so long hoped that I'd outgrow my disorder that they've convinced themselves that perhaps I actually have. Maybe I had, too, until my trip to Chicago, the night with the twins, and until I saw Chipper strapped into the toddler seat. Now that I've committed to taking care of the boys, am I beginning to realize just how little things have changed and how much it has limited my life?

No other bright, successful businesswoman I know avoids travel and hotels, dreads promotions and always buys expensive new pajamas because she never knows where she might be seen in them.

If Dr. Grant… I immediately put a stop to that train of thought. I know even he can't help. I've tried it all at least twice. Of course he *had* testified in the trials of murderers who suffered with parasomnias. He's a respected expert. Then a shiver of apprehension ran through me. I was jumping ahead of myself. I didn't even know for which side he testified. He probably helped send them all to jail.

I had mixed feelings when I picked up the mail and found a letter of congratulations on my new job position and a bundle of information they suggested I read while making ready to phase in to the new job as my predecessor phased out.

Be careful what you wish for—you might get it.

On the way to the airport, I stopped at rescue headquarters, a simple, unassuming building that was formerly a family-run service station. It was the best, cheapest location we could find for our last-chance facility. Since volunteers took many of the animals into their homes, we had eked by with limited space. The problem was that every time I stopped by I usually ended up taking home a new foster dog or cat. Sometimes I have four or five furry or feathered miscreants, orphans and runaways in my house at one time. Having only two, Chipper and Hammie, is a rarity for me.

This time, however, would be different. It would be easier to foster a team of sled dogs than my two nephews and there was no way on earth, after I turned Chipper over to his new home, that I would accept another animal until Mickey and Jeff returned.

I'm in denial, of course. That is like saying I won't eat chocolate again until I fit into the dress I wore to my junior prom. It just isn't going to happen.

"Hey, Suze, I hear you found a home for Chipper," Charley Cousins greeted me cheerfully. "Good job."

I smile every time I see Charley. He's got such passion for whatever he does that he throws himself into it a hundred and fifty percent. He's idealistic, intense and impossible to say no to when he really wants something to happen. That's why he's so good at what he does.

Charley's life follows two tracks. One involves animal rescue, the other, the theater—edgy, improvisational stuff. Even though Charley explains it to me completely before I attend, I've never been able to understand it. It does, however, explain why his hair is currently done in a bright green Mohawk and why lavish parrot-colored stripes are painted along both sides of his shaved head.

"Are you playing a bird in a stage version of *Doctor Dolittle* or modeling jungle wear for that clothing designer friend of yours?" I asked, helping myself to a handful of M&M's the colors of Charley's head. Eating chocolate already. Could a new pet be far behind?

"Jane has moved on. She's no longer doing jungle wear. She's into a retro stage, the sixties and seventies. Sort of Austin Powers meets the Waltons. I'm doing a skit for elementary-school kids on the importance of saving the rainforests and all its residents." He made a squawking sound like a parrot. "How do you like it?"

"It's perfect…if you are a parrot. How's it going to be when you try to grow it out?"

Charley tossed his head disdainfully but his

green Mohawk didn't budge. "I plan to do this for several weeks. Then I'll just shave my head and let it grow out naturally."

"Or you could paint it black and do a skit on the health benefits of bowling."

"Har, har. What are you here for? You didn't come just to torment me, did you?"

"No, just checking in. Is it a go to give Chipper to the woman we discussed?"

"She's a perfect match. She's going to call you in a couple days about when to pick him up."

We thoroughly check out every adoptive pet owner. These animals do not need another rejection or to be put in homes where they might be frightened or harmed again.

"Good. He's turned into a great little dog." I thought of him in bed with the twins. "I'm going to miss him."

"Not for long. As soon as Chipper goes to his new owner, you can pick up Chester."

Chester?

"No, I can't. I'm taking three months off. I'm babysitting for my sister's twins while she and her husband are in South America."

"The Demolition Derby Boys? No kidding?"

Charley's met the twins. The memories have never left him.

"You know I'd never subject an animal to them. Even though they play gently with Chipper and treat him like gold, I don't want to risk it."

"You may have to. Otherwise we don't know what to do with this guy. You are his last, best hope."

"Don't do that to me, Charley. I just can't take another dog right now."

"Oh, this isn't a dog. It's a cat."

"Oh, no you don't! No cats. I've done my time with them. Remember the time that one took up residence in my ceiling fan? I couldn't use the light in my living room for weeks. And the one that hauled my Thanksgiving turkey—which was triple its weight, by the way—off the table and onto the floor? Oh, yes, and the one that found its life passion was shredding my panty hose?"

"So you've had some feisty ones, that's all. You loved them all, haven't you? And their new owners simply adore them. Cats are wonderful pets."

"I don't disagree with you. I just can't take one right now. I'm not even feeding and housing strays anymore. I had to lay down the law. I've started chasing them away. No strays are allowed to enter my home until the boys are gone. Including this…Chester…or whoever he is."

He raised one eyebrow and his bald head creased, moving the Mohawk slightly.

"They can't even be in your yard?"

I took another handful of chocolate. This conversation was making me nervous. "Well, they can hang around outside if they like. It's a free country."

"And you don't feed them?"

"No, I don't…at least not anything good. Just some dry generic stuff I buy at the farm supply store."

"Dry-as-dust food? No water. How do they swallow?"

"There's water, of course. And, if I feel like it," I admitted reluctantly, "I soften the food with a little warm milk."

"And how often do you 'feel' like it? All of the time? Some of the time? Most of the time?" He sounded like a quiz from an *Oprah* magazine.

"Certainly not all the time."

"I see." How anyone whose head is painted to look like a parrot can make me feel guilty is beyond me, but Charley did.

"I usually don't get time on Fridays."

"So you do warm their food Saturday through Thursday?"

"I suppose so."

"And no treats, I imagine."

"Of course not!" Except for allowing them to have the juicy bits left over in the tuna can after I make my lunch.

"You sound like a real drill sergeant, Suze. I think you can handle this cat for a few days and manage the twins as well. After all, you don't have to get attached to it. You don't need to let it think that your house could possibly be its permanent home."

"I won't have time to work with it, Charley. This isn't like the other times. I won't be able to sit around and pet it or pick it up when it meows."

"I wouldn't even dream of expecting it. I *want* you to ignore it. No playing, no petting and certainly no cuddling. It's the best thing for all involved, except the cat, of course."

"The twins…"

"Are top priority. The cat will be no trouble at all, I'm sure."

"It will have to stay in the basement or my garage. No fooling, Charley. I won't have it lolling around on my furniture."

"So I can drop it by one night soon?"

"I'm not kidding this time, Charley. I will not make a fuss over this animal."

"Done."

As I got into my car to drive away, the import

of the conversation hit me. How had *that* happened? I told Charley *no* at every turn and he still thinks he's delivering a cat to my house.

Darla, looking like a contemporary Marilyn Monroe with her blond curls and I, exhausted and looking more like Ebenezer Scrooge, arrived at the doors outside baggage claim at the same time. She flung her overnight case into the back of my car and hopped in.

"Isn't this exciting? I'm going to ask the Realtor if there's anything near you. I'd like a townhome or a condo, of course. I don't have a string of critters living with me all the time so I don't need a house."

I smiled at her benevolently. "Don't hurry into that decision yet. A pet might be just the thing for you. By the way, I have a good friend I'd like you to meet. His name is Charley."

Chapter Eight

"What do you want for dinner? Takeout? Eat-in? Leftovers?" I asked.

"The question is, what do *you* want. I have strict instructions to take you out for dinner. Somewhere nice."

I laughed and blurted out the name of a steak house known for its blue-cheese shrimp, prime rib and garlic mashed potatoes. I knew it mostly for its prices.

"Done. Let's go there."

"Are you kidding? We can eat for a week on what you'll pay for dinner there."

"I have my orders," Darla said stubbornly. "The main office is very fond of you, Suze, and…" Her voice trailed away.

"And what?"

"Nothing. I told them there was nothing to worry about."

"Now you have to tell me." I pulled onto I-94 and headed west but was too busy with traffic to glare at her.

"They just have—" she searched for a word "—a feeling about you. They want me to make sure you're happy."

"What do you mean 'feeling?'"

Huge trucks sped by me in the lanes on either side of my car.

"Get us to the restaurant and I'll explain. You need to pay attention to your driving."

"So this is what it is going to be like with you back in the Cities. Nag, boss, nag."

She giggled. "Yes. Isn't it wonderful?"

We pulled into the driveway of the rugged stone building and a valet appeared out of thin air.

"No, I'll just…"

"We'll take valet parking, Suze," Darla said firmly. "Like I said, the company has…"

"I know, a *feeling*." I handed my keys to the young man, not without relief. The parking lot was filled with Mercedes, Porsches, BMWs and the occasional Acura, Saab or Volvo. Not cars I wanted to accidentally back into or leave with a dent.

Inside, we were greeted and spirited to a table near a window, given menus and a spiel of the many and varied special dishes the chef was concocting tonight. Before I could speak, Darla ordered appetizers, soup, salad, entrées and requested to see the dessert cart.

"We'll be here all night," I pointed out. "And some-one will have to roll us to our car on a furniture dolly. Did the company send you here because they thought I was too thin?"

"My immediate superior was on the interview team. They felt that although you were perfect for the job and seemed to want it, something was holding you back."

So they had picked up on my reservations at the interview.

"Did you tell them what it was?"

"I wanted to talk to you first. Suze, you will have to explain to them your issue with traveling."

The gaping pit in my stomach grew a little wider. "It's never going to go away, is it? These sleep issues are going to haunt me for the rest of my life." I took a sip of water and stared across the room filled with well-dressed people who all appeared relaxed and festive. I'm not a jealous person but envy momentarily swamped me. None of them had to consider turning down jobs because of something so ridiculous as sleepwalking! Why me?

The answer is, of course, why *not* me? My grandmother always said that if everyone in the world threw their troubles into a pile and then picked new ones, many would likely take their own troubles back. She's probably right. There are far more grievous issues than mine out there.

"Suze?" Darla was looking at me with a frown on her face. "Are you okay?"

"Yes. I'm just frustrated. I want the job, Darla. I've been thinking of hiring someone to travel with me and be my night watchman." There, I'd said it. My answer to my worst-case scenario. Then I told her about my experience with the twins.

She sat there, moving her appetizers around the plate with her fork. "Why don't you try the medical route again?"

"I've done it all, Darla. The only way I stay put at night is if I'm so medicated that I can't function the next day. I can't begin to tell you how much I hated that. I felt groggy and listless all the time. My judgment was poor, I was dangerous behind the wheel of a car. I wasn't *me*."

"Maybe there's new stuff on the market...." Darla's voice trailed off.

"I don't think anyone can help me."

She looked up and stared across the room with an odd expression on her features. "No one? What about that doctor you met at the hotel in Chicago? He lives here, right?"

"I can see a million problems with that one, Darla. Besides, he doesn't personally take patients anymore." *And I could never look him in the eye again. He'd witnessed one of my more bizarre sleepwalking episodes to date.* Clouds and sheep, ice cubes, laments and pleas toward heaven. But I hadn't told Darla about that. No, he'd already seen enough of me.

"You said he's opening a clinic. Maybe he could have one of his people talk to you."

"What do you want me to do? Call him? Appear on his doorstep? Get real, Darla, I'll never see him again."

"I don't think you should be so sure about that." She smiled at me oddly.

I glanced up to see where she'd been looking so intently. On the far side of the room, looking impossibly handsome in dark trousers, an immaculate white shirt and trim brown tweed suit coat was David Grant. He was part of a larger group, I could see, but he was laughing and talking with a leggy brunette who seemed to hang on his every word. Then a petite blonde touched his arm and he turned his considerable charisma on her. The other men in the group were equally good-looking, but Dr. Grant seemed to have a corner on the charm market—and the women.

"So what? Do you think I'm going to walk over there and say 'Excuse me, but could you help me quit sleepwalking?'"

"He's a sleep doctor, Suze, he's seen people lots crazier than you, I'm sure."

I didn't know how to respond to that. Fortunately our entrées arrived and Darla turned her attention from the man across the room to the feast in front of her.

By the time we were done with the main course, I was so full that I had trouble rolling my eyeballs. Darla, on the other hand, was only getting started.

"Coffee with cream," she ordered. "A piece of bread pudding with caramel sauce, key lime pie and some of the flourless chocolate cake, please. And to-go boxes for the leftovers."

I eyed the pile of boxes we'd already filled. I'd be eating well for a week. Darla with an expense account is a extraordinary thing to experience. Even after we'd sampled the desserts and received our coffee with cream, Darla seemed in no hurry to leave the restaurant.

It was I who was getting restless. I did not want to run into David Grant and had kept my face averted since Darla first pointed him out.

Even that I found depressing. Most people who are ashamed to look someone in the eye were at least awake for their transgression. I, on the other hand, make a much better fool of myself in my sleep.

"I have something to admit to you," Darla murmured. Now it was her turn to avert her eyes. She stirred her coffee studiously. "It's not much but I think I should tell you."

"What did you do, Darla?" I felt suddenly apprehensive.

"I looked up Dr. Grant on the internet. I decided that even if you wouldn't pursue this, I would." She rummaged in her purse. "I was going to give this to you later but since he's here and we're talking about him, now's the time." She pulled out several folded sheets of paper and thrust them across the table to me.

I pushed them back toward her. "I don't need to see it."

"Oh, but you do." She unfolded the pages and shoved them at me. "Read."

Reluctantly I picked up the papers. "Renowned sleep disorders group to open a clinic under the leadership of famed neurologist and sleep researcher, Dr. David Grant, who has accepted the position of medical director. Grant brings years of experience in working with sleep disorders and doing clinical research to the position.

"Grant Research, Inc. will provide state-of-the-art testing, board-certified physicians, highly trained technologists, medical personnel and cutting-edge programs. Under Dr. Grant's leadership, it is believed that this research facility and treatment center could become one of the outstanding facilities in the nation.

"'Only a small percentage of individuals with sleep disorders are diagnosed and treated,'" says Dr. Grant. "'It's my mission to raise that percentage and provide a better, easier life for the many individuals struggling with this issue.'"

"So?" I tried to sound casual but my heart was pounding in my chest. I experienced a feeling that had long been absent where my sleep disorder was concerned—hope.

"This is your chance, Suze. And you've already met! It will be easy to reconnect."

Right. Easy. As soon as I have a lobotomy and forget what happened between us.

Unfortunately David arrived at our table before I could get it scheduled.

He looked even better than I remembered. That's amazing since what I remember was pretty remarkable.

"Ms. Charles?" he inquired politely. His eyes crinkled pleasantly at the corners. I recalled him as I'd seen him that night in the hotel—elegantly dressed, calm, amused but compassionate and I wished we'd met under any other circumstances. Why couldn't I have had a flat tire in his presence? Or fallen down a flight of stairs? Something that, if not graceful, at least wasn't completely weird.

Too late to hide now however; might as well blunder through it. "Hello, Dr. Grant."

I introduced Darla, who was kicking me under the table. She bestowed on him one of her brightest, most entrancing smiles. As I looked at David through my friend's eyes, I understood why she was batting her eyelashes and playing the Southern belle even though she was about as Southern as the Canadian border.

Then, much to my dismay, Darla craned her neck as if looking for someone standing near the door to the ladies' restroom. Uh-oh. Suddenly she began to wave and stood up from her chair. "I think I see someone I might know. Dr. Grant, it's so nice to meet you. Please, stay and visit with Suze while I check this out." And she steamed off purposefully, apparently determined to find this mysterious acquaintance of hers.

It was an old trick, something my friends had devised in college for discretely getting out of the way when one of us was talking to a good-looking guy. "Evacuate the area," one of the girls would whisper and abruptly everyone was sure they recognized someone they knew in other parts of the room. It was also a clear signal that the guy in question had their mark of approval. We never left a friend alone with a guy of whom we didn't approve.

Dr. Grant was as good as wearing Darla's endorsement on his forehead now.

"Any more episodes?" he asked gently. "Or would you rather not talk about it?"

"Things are fine, thanks." I closed my eyes against the image of Chipper strapped into Tommy's car seat. "Nothing unusually abnormal." Unfortunately I was telling the complete, honest truth about that. Once I'd trimmed all the shrubs in my parents' front yard during a midnight gardening frenzy.

He had to have felt the chilly wall I erected between us but he was gracious nonetheless.

"This is a pleasant surprise." He glanced at one of the empty chairs at the table.

Not too obvious or anything, I thought. "Would you like to sit down?"

"Thanks. Don't mind if I do."

As he slid into the chair, I wondered what was wrong with me. The best looking, probably most intelligent man in the room was making nice with me and I was miserable about it.

"Do you come here often?" he asked, using the oldest line in the book. "It's one of my favorite places to eat. They have great ribs and the desserts are excellent."

I didn't admit that the prices were a little steep for me. They obviously didn't make a dent in his billfold.

"I know." I indicated the to-go boxes. "I had several."

"Remember the diner we went to in Chicago? That's my other favorite spot."

I'd nearly forgotten. "It was rather amazing, wasn't it? I believe I ate the world's finest breakfast in that little place."

I hardly noticed Darla drift back into the picture. Dr. Grant was regaling me with a story of the time he'd had to break up a fight between the cook and a biker who had accused the cook of over-salting the eggs. Not only that, mesmerized as I was by his dark good looks, I wasn't interested in looking around the room when the scenery was so pleasant here.

There were flecks of black in his irises that gave them more depth and mystery than I'd observed when I'd first met him. They were eyes worth staring into.

"…you'll never believe it!" Darla babbled. "It *was* Janet Halder. Remember her? We worked together for three years. It is so much fun to see her. She asked us to come back to her place for dessert. What do you think?"

"We've already had three desserts. Where would I put a fourth—in my shoe?"

"Just for a little bit? Janet and I have a lot of catching up to do."

"Why don't you drop me off at my place and then take the car? I don't mind."

"Why don't you take Suze's car, and *I'll* take her home."

We both turned to stare at Dr. Grant. He shrugged. "I'm happy to do it. Suze and I have already shared one interesting experience. I'd like to get to know her better." He looked me square in the eye and I was like a walleye with a jig and a minnow dangling in front of me. Caught.

Chapter Nine

Our ride home was exceedingly uncomfortable—for me, at least. David seemed perfectly at ease behind the wheel of his BMW.

"My grandmother lived in this part of town," he commented as we neared my home. "I have fond memories of visiting her here. Her house always smelled like baking bread."

"Is she gone now?"

"From the Twin Cities. She bought a penthouse condo in Florida and lives on the ocean."

"Yay, Granny," I murmured.

David laughed out loud. "I agree entirely. At eighty she walks the beach with her bulldog Esther and plays bridge four nights a week. My grandmother created a life she loves."

I felt a sudden irrational jealousy for David's grandmother. She'd taken charge of her life.

Why hadn't I, who was fifty years younger, been able to do so?

Because if I lived on the top floor in a high-rise building I'd probably get out of bed one night, decide to walk a nonexistent dog off my patio and take a very long first step.

My house, with its plethora of gingerbread and a wide wraparound porch, came into view. I chose this house because it radiates my favorite quality in a home—cozy. It speaks to my personality. Fluffy throws, puffy pillows, hot chocolate, sleeping puppies, bubble baths, warm towels and tea parties—that's me. Because I sometimes feel like a captive in my own house, the least I can do is make it a velvet prison.

"Here we are." I opened the car door and practically fell out before he stopped the car.

David hurried out to help me, the perfect gentleman.

I wanted to run inside and close the door behind me but my good upbringing got in the way.

"Thanks for the ride." The man did bring me home. Deciding not to make him think I'm any wackier than I already am, with a sigh, I added, "Would you like to come inside? I make a pretty good cup of hot cocoa."

There was no hesitation. "Thank you, I'd love to."

As we walked into the house I did a quick mental inventory of how I'd left it. I'm normally a tidy person but I also have a number of hobbies and collections that are not always easy to rein in. This week I'd been piecing a quilt and doing decorative painting on a set of straight-backed chairs I'd found at a garage sale. Mickey says it's my nature to try to save everything—animals, furniture, scraps of fabric and anything lonely or neglected.

She might be right, I realized as we walked into the house and I recalled that today's rescue mission had been the birds who feed on my deck and occasionally get disoriented and attempt to fly into my picture window. Two or three had knocked themselves silly only this morning and, because I have no curtains to draw on that particular window, I'd done the next best thing—taped long strips of toilet paper to the tops of the windows. They drifted in the air from my forced-air heating system, creating enough movement and texture to warn the birds not to fly in that direction. It appeared that someone had T-P-ed the inside of my house.

That would have been bad enough, but I'd

also spread newspapers on the floor and set the primed chairs in the center of the room and begun painting swirling vines on the legs and backs of them. My idea was to create a jungle theme. I'd tried to paint a roaring lion on the seat of one but the unfortunate lion's mouth got too wide and his teeth too long. Regrettably the result was that the chair looked like it would devour—bottom first—anyone who tried to sit in it.

And then there were the mustache cups. Mickey calls it odd, but ever since I was a child, I've been fascinated with mustaches. I don't like them on the men I date, but I have fond memories of my late grandfather's bushy mustache. I was particularly intrigued by the concept of a cup meant to keep his mustache dry with an extra bit of porcelain stretched across the cup so that the drinker could sip through the small opening it provided and protect his mustache at the same time. As kids, we'd scoured neighborhood rummage sales for the things and had come home with several cracked and chipped "antiques."

Grandmother made sure that when Grandfather died I inherited those cups and, for some bizarre reason, also his shaving brushes. My grandfather's old-fashioned ways left me with shaving brushes, razor strops and empty bottles of Old Spice.

I'd decided it was time to clear out my odd-ball collection and there were cracked cups, brushes and strops scattered all over my coffee table. And if that weren't enough, I'd baked yesterday and filled my collection of clown cookie jars with oatmeal-raisin, chocolate-chip and macadamia-nut white-chocolate cookies. The jars were still sitting on the counter beaming out at me with painted smiles, triangle eyebrows and large bow ties.

I was used to such chaos but if I imagined looking through David's eyes, it must seem as if he'd walked into a weird and freaky fun house at a surreal carnival.

And then Hammie, sensing my discomfort, began to race around on his squeaky wheel and Chipper careened on three legs into David's ankles, took hold of his pant leg with his razor-sharp teeth and began to growl, obviously channeling a Rottweiler.

"Welcome to my home," I said meekly. This might turn out all right after all. After this experience, David would never want to drive me home or even darken my doorstep again.

Thanks to his good breeding, David didn't

flinch, although his eyes did widen when Chipper let go of his pant leg and tried to take a bite out of his highly polished shoe.

"Sorry about this. I didn't know I was getting company."

"Don't apologize. This is one of the most… interesting…homes I've ever seen."

I'll bet.

Chipper returned to gnawing on his pant leg. David, dragging the dog with him, moved toward the chairs. "You have a lot of talent."

"You are too kind. If I had talent, that lion would not look like it was going to eat alive the first person who sat on its face." I whisked the chairs out of the way, gathered the newspapers in my arm and nodded toward a pair of red chairs. "Have a seat."

He dropped into the nearest chair, suppressing a sigh.

That will teach him to get involved with me, I thought wearily. Even I am confused when dealing with me.

I left him to absorb the atmosphere while I heated milk for hot chocolate. He seemed happy to see something familiar—china cups and a plate of fresh cookies— when I returned.

"It's not surprising I walk in my sleep, is it?" I asked. "When I look around here I realize that my waking life and my dream state are equally bizarre."

"Hardly." He eyed the cup in my hand. "If anything were to keep you awake it would probably be caffeine at 10:00 p.m."

"Isn't cocoa supposed to put me to sleep?"

He didn't answer. He just said, "I like your house. It's cozy."

"Cluttered."

"Warm and inviting. Unique."

"I'll give you that. It is interesting. And it will look much better once I get rid of the mustache cups, finish the chairs and give the dog away."

"Pardon me? Give your dog away?"

"He's not my dog. Not really. I'm his foster mother."

Now David looked really confused. "I didn't know. Is it a government program?"

I couldn't help but smile. "I wish it were. We could use the funding." And I told him about the rescue center and the dozens of animals I'd "mothered" over the years.

"Chipper has a new home. He'll be leaving here next week. The woman is very excited to have him and I think it will be a great match."

"Won't you miss him?"

"Of course, but there is always another neglected or rejected animal to foster."

"What will you get next?"

"Nothing, if I can help it." I planned to reject Charley and Chester the cat when they got to my door. "The director thinks he has an animal for me but for the next two or three months I'll be watching my twin nephews while my sister goes to South America to adopt a baby. That will be problem enough."

David is a wonderful conversationalist and an even better listener. Without a bit of hesitation, I found myself telling him about Mickey and Jeff and their longing for another child.

"Would you like to see pictures of my nephews?" I volunteered.

We brought our beverages and a plate of my fresh cookies to the couch so I could sit beside him and show him the album of pictures of the boys.

"They're a handsome pair," David commented. "I don't know if I've ever seen a cuter set of twins."

"That's part of the problem. Because they are so cute and have the look of little angels with tarnished halos, they get away with far more than they should. That combined with unquenchable energy, cunning intelligence and the slyness of a pair of fox pups, their parents never had a chance."

"Never?"

"Tommy loves to pound, pummel, clobber, bash, hammer, crush and pulverize. He's our he-man twin. Terry, on the other hand, has remarkable managerial skills. He'll be a CEO someday, I'm sure of it."

"So Terry is the brains and Tommy, the brawn?"

"A perfect combination for whipping a perfectly lovely but inexperienced set of parents into compliance, lunacy and servitude without them ever seeing it coming."

"How do they get away with it?" David inquired, obviously enjoying our discussion. Of course, David enjoys many things I wouldn't have expected. He's very down to earth and approachable for someone with his position in life. I'll bet his patients never feel like lab rats.

"They are also incredibly funny." I offered him the cookie plate again. "So funny, in fact, that it's difficult to keep from bursting into laughter even though you really *didn't* want your refrigerator cleaned and the contents fed to the dog."

"Are you bragging or complaining?" he asked bluntly.

"A little of both. When we're not crying, we're laughing."

I was enjoying this a little too much, I realized. I was doing a terrible job of avoiding David. My resolve to put the episode we shared behind me was fading and I didn't want that to happen. Next thing I knew he'd be trying to talk me back into the circus maze of tests and medications I was determined to avoid. That thought made me very nervous.

Hammie, detecting my anxiety—I haven't had a handsome man in my house for a very long time, after all—began to whirr on his wheel with greater and greater speed. If his foot slipped and he were not in a cage, he could have propelled himself across the room with momentum alone.

David's smile became more and more strained as the racket grew, until finally he stood up. "I have some mechanical skills, maybe you'd like me to look at that hamster's wheel." The expression on his face said, *Or else.*

I lifted Hammie out of his cage and held him close to my chest as David did minor surgery on the offending wheel. The hamster's heart was pounding so hard that it felt as if it might pump right through his rib cage and fur and land in my hand.

I know the feeling, buddy. I know the feeling.

"There, let him try this." David dusted his hands together and shredded paper and hay bedding flew off his fingers.

I swear I saw an expression of surprise on Hammie's face when he jumped on the wheel and there was no sound other than a soft, pleasant whirr. No clanking, no rattling, no sounding as if he were going to run his entire cage off its table. After a few moments, the whirr made Hammie relax since he dozed off midstride, tumbled off the wheel and went to sleep.

"Bravo!" I clapped politely. "Hammie thanks you."

"Believe me, the pleasure was all mine. How could you stand that racket, by the way?"

I dropped down on the sofa beside him again. "I've learned to tolerate a lot in my life. I accept things as they are. I tried to fix the wheel dozens of times and then I quit and decided to learn to live with it."

He studied me intently with those deep dark eyes that seemed to melt my skin and see all the way into my soul. "The same way you decided to learn to live with your sleep disorder rather than try to get more help?"

"When you are disappointed often enough, you just start to cope." One thing I'm good at is coping.

"Did you have anyone else try to fix the hamster wheel?"

"Several people, but none of them had your touch."

"Just like the other doctors you saw who tried and failed you, Suze? What if I'm the one with the 'touch' you've been looking for?"

"I'm not a hamster wheel, David."

"What are you afraid of, Suze? Why did you give up?"

Why *had* I?

After a moment's consideration I said, "Frankly? Odd as it may sound, I got sick and tired of being a guinea pig. If I slept poorly without electrodes attached to my head, imagine how badly I did *with* them. I and the pharmacist were on a first-name basis and I had to devote an entire shelf to drugs I'd tried and that had failed. Every new drug on the market came my way first. The only other thing I could have done was work for the FDA. I spent years as a walking zombie. Granted, I slept at night, but I also slept during the day with my eyes wide open. I can't even *remember* my own sister's wedding because of whatever 'miracle drug' they'd put me on. I refuse to live my life that way any longer."

He looked at me with compassion, something my friends and family had almost run out of. "When you're ready, Suze, I'll be here. Although I now just consult with other doctors, I can provide you with recommendations…."

Infuriatingly, tears sprang to my eyes. Where were you five years ago, Dr. Grant, when I still had that rare commodity of hope? And, more exasperating yet, why aren't you saying you'll wait for me and not for my disorder?

Dr. Grant and me. Wouldn't that be ironic? The sleep-disorder doctor and the patient he can't cure? No way. I refuse to get myself into a situation where the man I care about views me as his biggest failure.

I glanced at Hammie's cage. Astoundingly, he was still asleep. If he were aware of the way I was feeling, he should have been running at warp speed on his wheel. Maybe he wasn't as attuned to my emotional weather as I'd given him credit for being.

Chapter Ten

After Hammie's clatter was silenced and Chipper let go of David's pant leg and jumped onto his lap instead, things settled down. My fresh cookies were a hit. They were just like his grandmother's, David said with great relish.

"Your home is very comfortable and inviting," he commented after polishing off a half-dozen cookies.

"And…"

He grinned. "Granted, it's a little disconcerting at first, but that wears off rather quickly."

Honesty. I can accept that.

"Tell me more about yourself," I encouraged. "I know so little about you."

He shrugged as if he and his history were of little importance. "There's nothing much. I grew up on a farm in Michigan. I have a sister who is in medicine and a brother who is still managing the family farm."

If this is the kind of farm boy Michigan grows, it's my new favorite state.

"As I indicated, I have a Southern grandmother who still mistrusts the 'Yankees' but has done her best to instill me with gracious manners despite my suspect northern upbringing."

He mentioned a pedigreed list of educational institutions and then, probably because of his grandmother's teaching, began to ask me questions about myself.

I kicked off my shoes, curled my legs beneath me and sank into the deep cushions of my couch. David stood to remove his suit jacket and toss it over the back of a chair. My knees brushed his thigh as we sat together on the couch. I hadn't felt so at home inside myself in days.

"As a neurologist, how did you become interested in studying sleep disorders? Surely there are more glamorous issues with the brain than that."

"Glamour? I suppose you could put it that way, but I wanted to research something that would make a difference in the lives of as many people as possible. Once I saw the numbers on how many people actually suffer from different parasomnias, I made up my mind. *Parasomnias* is the umbrella name for disorders that interrupt the sleep process and create troublesome sleep-related events. They include arousal disorders, sleep-wake transition disorders and poor REM sleep, most of which, by the way, you exhibit."

Thanks a bunch, I thought. I was worried for a minute that I'd missed one.

"It's fascinating, really. What really caught my attention was learning about fatal familial insomnia while I was in medical school."

"*Fatal?* Isn't that a bit of an exaggeration?"

"Not at all. It's very rare, but it exists. It's caused by an inherited gene that sends the patient into complete sleeplessness. It's untreatable and therefore ultimately fatal. There are only a few families in the world that suffer from it but they literally die from insomnia."

"And I thought I had it bad," I murmured.

He reached for another cookie. "I realized that this was a way I could help to ease a lot of people's stress. The general public doesn't necessarily see a sleep disorder as life-altering, but, as you know, it can be."

"Boy, do I know." I'd had no intention of talking about this, but the man had already seen me in an episode, so there wasn't much to hide.

"You saw firsthand why I worry about traveling. My new job will involve much more of it."

"And, I'm guessing, you've even considered not taking it for that very reason."

I punched my fist into a thick crewel-embroidered pillow on my couch. "Yes, unfortunately I have. But I can't put my life on hold any longer." I heard my voice crack. "I just can't."

What makes it worse is that I feel intuitively that there is no help for me. It isn't just my biological clock that's ticking rapidly these days. I can see my entire life slipping away while I cocoon myself in cotton batting and protect myself from the world. And, considering what I do in my sleep, the world from me.

"Nor should you have to."

"David, I know what you're thinking but forget it. I've tried. And now I've quit trying. It's been an exercise in frustration, humiliation and disappointment. I've learned to manage."

"As long as you are in the confines of your own home and can make sure that nothing happens to you or anyone else in the night."

Without warning, a feeling of stark terror washed over me. I could give up the job. I could lock myself in the house. But what I couldn't do was let my sister down. Mickey could have separated the boys so that her child-care people *could* play one-on-one rather than be double-teamed, but for two months or more? What kind of trauma would that cause not only for the boys but for their parents?

"What just happened?" David asked softly. "Your expression looked like you'd just seen a ghost—or a monster."

"I suppose I did," I admitted reluctantly. "I saw myself trying to care for my nephews alone for two or three months." I straightened, metaphorically stiffening my spine. "I guess it just means that I hire someone to stay with me at night and babysit for the three of us. My friend Darla will help me out, I'm sure."

"Or you could get help and do it alone."

I held up a hand in protest. "Haven't you heard me?"

"I have. All I'm saying is that I'm here if you need me."

I stared at his handsome, troubled face.

Oh, David, if you only knew how much I've wished some man would say that to me! But it has to be about me, not the curious disorder that makes me feel like a side-show freak.

Our conversation dwindled and died after that and soon David stood up.

"Thanks for everything. I had a great time."

"Slumming, you mean?"

"Visiting a house of unique adventures and wondrous delights," he corrected, smiling. He peered at Hammie, who was comatose in his cage. "I've had more fun here than at a dozen boring parties where everyone wants to tell me their problems and have me diagnose them on the spot."

"Ewww. I see your problem. No one ever asks me to evaluate their insurance claims over canapés. How do you handle that?"

He grinned and I saw beneath his sophisticated exterior to his boyish charm. "Mostly, I ask them to take their clothes off and lie down on the dining-room table so I can examine them. That usually cuts them off at the pass."

"You don't!"

"No, but you don't know how many times I've been tempted." He took my hand. It nestled nicely into his larger one. "I've had a good time tonight, Suze. I hope our paths cross again."

He didn't make sure of that, however, because he didn't ask me to go out again. He no doubt meant to see me in his office but he'd have a very long wait for that.

"Thank you." David leaned forward and kissed my cheek.

Thank *you*, I thought as I watched the tail-lights of his car disappear around the corner of my block.

My work phone rang at 10:00 a.m. the next morning.

"Suze, it's Mickey. Am I disturbing you?"

"Not at all. I've been here since 5:00 a.m. It's time for a break."

"Didn't you sleep last night? Or were you sleepwalking?"

"Neither. I just had a lot on my mind so I decided to come to work early."

Actually, I had Dr. David Grant on my mind. Some sleep doctor he is. Thinking about him kept me awake all night.

"Are you sitting down?"

"Yes," I said suspiciously. "Why?"

"Because we're going to South America tomorrow! We've just heard that they may be willing to speed up the process if we leave tomorrow. It is only a couple days earlier than we'd planned. We changed our plane reservations to 6:00 a.m. tomorrow. We have to be at the airport three hours early for an international flight. That means we'll have to leave our house by 2:30 a.m. Do you want to sleep at our place tonight so we don't have to wake the boys or would you rather have them at your house?"

Where there are locks on the doors to prevent the lunatic from escaping.

"My place," I said automatically, still processing this horrific bit of information. Reality was setting in. By this time tomorrow the boys would be mine, all mine.

"Oh, Suze, this is it! This is the first step toward getting our little girl!" Mickey started to cry. "I can't believe it's finally happening."

Me either. I don't have a babysitter lined up for *me* yet.

"What time will you be over with them?"

"Bedtime. Jeff and I want to tuck them in and explain why we won't be there when they wake up in the morning."

Oh, Lord, I prayed silently, *just let* me *be there when they wake up and not wandering around the neighborhood.*

"Oh, darling, I'm sorry Dad and I can't help you," Mom said apologetically when I called her. "Did you forget, your father has a dental convention in Miami this week? We're taking Mickey and Jeff to the airport and then just waiting for our own plane. Isn't it nice that it worked out that way?"

"Maybe Darla can help. She called to say that she was going to spend tonight in a hotel because of the location of her morning meetings. I'd just like someone here a day or two until we all get acclimated."

"You worry too much, Suze. After all, you've practically outgrown your sleepwalking now, haven't you?"

De Nile is not just a river in Egypt.

My mother is so far into denial, in fact, that she actually almost believes what she's saying. I don't have the heart to burst her bubble again. As long as I don't talk about what happens at night, she thinks that nothing is going on. At least she sleeps better that way.

"Tonight?" Darla wailed into the phone. "Oh, Suze, I can't. I'm going out with one of the district managers to several small towns. We're leaving early and he lives on the northwest side of the Cities so that's where I'm staying tonight. I don't want to ask him to drive all the way down to your place to pick me up."

"It is fine, Darla, don't worry. We'll be a-okay. I just wanted a little backup tonight, that's all. We're going to be fine, fine, fine."

And if I believe that, I have some swampland in Florida I'd like to sell myself.

Mickey and Jeff arrived at seven-thirty with

the boys, who smelled of soap and men's after-shave.

"I turned my back and they dumped the whole bottle on themselves," Jeff admitted. "It almost gags me, but they don't seem to mind how they smell. I suppose it will wear off eventually."

"Don't worry about it, they are washable." Having my house smell like the men's cologne department at Macy's is the least of my problems.

"But we *have* washed them."

Oh. Good thing I like Jean Paul Gaultier.

Mickey barely let me say hello to the little guys. She held them so tightly she reminded me of a benevolent boa constrictor so I stayed out of her way.

When the boys were tucked in and sound asleep, she came into the kitchen with tears running down her cheeks.

"How am I going to feel without them?"

Relieved? But I didn't say it out loud.

"Think of the new baby, of the wonderful family you'll have."

Mickey snuffled like an elephant with a head cold and threw her arms around me.

"Take care of them, Suze? Just like I would? You are my sister and they love you almost as much as they love me."

Okay, good. Put even more responsibility on my shoulders.

"You know it, sis."

After several minutes of emotional blubbering, Jeff was able to pry my sister off me and shoo her out the door. I could see her sobbing as they drove away.

I paced the floor after they left, the full weight of responsibility lying heavy on my shoulders.

Frankly, without backup, I realized that I didn't *dare* go to sleep. What if…What if….

I couldn't let my sister down.

Therefore, I baked more cookies, painted the other wooden chair with a rhinoceros's gaping maw on the seat of this one, made a shadow box of my grandfather's shaving equipment and stored away the rest, and finished every bit of office work I could do on my computer. I also purchased new pots and pans and a collectible porcelain doll on QVC.

It was with huge relief when I heard Tommy and Terry padding from their room into the kitchen the next morning. They, at least, had survived the night.

What's more, they were even cuter than when they'd gone to sleep. Both boys covered my face with wet, delighted-to-see-you kisses, ate toast with peanut butter and jalapeño jelly, a combination they'd discovered by accident at my mother's house, and went happily to the babysitter where they would stay during the day.

I, on the other had, was not cute at all. My eyes were bloodshot, my hair stringy because I ran out of time getting the boys ready and couldn't shower and my exhaustion was as apparent as my pathetic hairdo.

I fell asleep twice in my office, once over the top of my computer, somehow deleting most of the work I'd done. The other time, I dozed off in my chair but woke up on the floor under my desk. Fortunately, everyone who'd come looking for me had not looked down and assumed I was out doing company business.

Five o'clock came far too soon, however. I had to pick up the boys and make it through the evening on those two brief naps.

Fortunately, Darla arrived at my door just at dinnertime to find the twins blowing bubbles in their soup with straws and me just plain foaming at the mouth.

Chapter Eleven

I've always scoffed at the idea of zombies and the hocus-pocus about the "walking dead" those misguided fans of horror movies seem to relish. That was, however, before I became one myself.

I haven't cleaned my bathroom in a week. That was when Darla returned to Chicago to wrap things up there and left me alone with the twins again. What's the use? The tidal wave that hits it every night when the boys take their bath will undo any polishing or scrubbing I might attempt. I don't know how, but the twins have managed to get water spots and soap scum not only on the ceiling but also inside closets and the medicine cabinet.

One evening, before I'd run their bathwater, I dashed to the laundry room to get clean towels. By the time I got back, they'd discovered a can of hair spray I hadn't placed high enough—like on the ceiling fixture perhaps—and sprayed it over the entire room.

Hair spray dries quickly. I know this for sure because when I walked into the room, the floor was like a sheet of thin black ice. My feet went out from under me, the towels flew in the air as I tried to right myself and as I fell, I felt my head smacking hard on the toilet bowl.

I couldn't have been out long because when I opened my eyes and slowly reached up to feel the goose egg on my scalp, Tommy and Terry were standing over me giggling.

"Auntie Suze hit the potty!" Tommy said, his eyes wide.

Children have a puzzling love for references to bathrooms and underwear. When Tommy said *potty*, Terry broke into gales of laugher. "Potty, potty, potty."

"Dotty, dotty, dotty," Tommy rhymed.

"Potty dotty, dotty potty." They fell on top of me giggling.

"Auntie Suze, she went dotty, yes indeed she hit the potty," I muttered.

I'm not much of a poet but the subject matter isn't all that profound either. I should be glad,

I suppose, that I didn't have a concussion or brain damage from the fall.

Or maybe I did.

I soldiered through bath time and our nightly rituals. Bath, stories, back rubs and finally, prayers. Those prayers are getting me through the day. If there is anything sweeter or more trusting than a child's prayer, I haven't discovered it yet.

"Now we lay us down to sleep... Bless Mommy, Daddy, our new baby sister in Souf Amerita, Grandma and Grandpa Charles, Grandma and Grandpa Martin, bless Hammie, bless Chipper..."

The list can sometimes be ten minutes long, especially if they start naming playmates and stuffed animals. I cling to the hope that they save the best for last.

"...and Auntie Suze who hit her head on the potty...."

"And now she's dotty!"

Yes, Lord, please do help me. If dotty is the worst I am by the time Mickey and Jeff get back, I'll be lucky.

The phone rang shortly after I returned to the living room feeling washed out as the towels I'd just thrown in the laundry. It was Darla.

"How's it going? Are you going to make it?"

"Oh, ye of little faith."

"Have you slept yet?"

I attempt to stay awake while the boys sleep. After the long night, I take them to the sitter as early as possible so that I can get an hour or two of shut-eye before I have to go to work. I do it in reverse in the afternoon, picking them up as late as I can, sleeping outside the babysitter's house in my car until the very last minute. I also try to get forty winks during my lunch hour. The schedule is wearing on me. I've already lost four pounds.

"I'm getting some sleep," I prevaricated.

"I'm sorry I can't be there with you. Since my moving plans got pushed back, it's been crazy here. If you can hang on a few more days, I'll be there to stay with you."

Hang on, Suze, hang on, like a shipwrecked sailor to a life raft in the ocean.

"I'm looking forward to it," I admitted. "A good night's sleep seems like an impossible dream."

"Don Quixote aside, I'm worried about you. You'll ruin your health trying to stay awake like this."

"But think of all the things I've gotten done."

I've organized my recipes, written letters to everyone I've ever known and a few I didn't, found a chat room full of insomniacs on the

Internet, seen every infomercial ever produced, purchased a new wardrobe on QVC and taught myself to crochet dishcloths from a how-to book. And that's not to mention that every drawer, closet and shelf in my house is immaculate. When I die of exhaustion and my family goes through my personal belongings, they'll be very impressed with how tidy I'd become.

"Go to see Dr. Grant, will you? He said he'd find you a physician at his clinic...."

"Gotta go, Darla. Talk to you soon."

"One of these days you're going to listen to me, Suze. Just don't wait until it's too late."

Too late for what? I wondered. As I faced another long, weary night, my curiosity got the best of me. What was that story David had told about a family who couldn't sleep?

The best and worst thing about the Internet is that everything you want to know—and even more that you don't—is at your fingertips.

Even though I knew better than to poke at a hornet's nest—the one in my mind—I searched *fatal familial insomnia.*

Words leaped off the screen like an assault against my complacence. "Increasing insomnia...panic attacks...hallucinations...rapid weight loss...dementia....doesn't show itself until or past childbearing years…." Maybe I was already in the fourth and last stage of the disease! Never mind that it's inherited and only twenty-eight families in the world suffer from it.

Now thoroughly depressed, I just dug myself deeper into the pit by searching for cases in which sleepwalking was used as a murder defense. *Homicidal somnambulism*, it was called, and the outcomes of the trials varied given the judges and juries.

It took a pint of chocolate-chip-cookie-dough ice cream, a half a jar of hot fudge topping eaten right with a spoon and three glasses of warm milk with cinnamon to settle me down. Maybe insomnia isn't so bad, considering the alternatives.

Now, too full to sleep, I wandered into the living room. The twins had demanded tonight to see pictures of me when I was their age and all my photo albums were strewn across the room. I'm eclectic in my photo management. That means whenever I have new pictures, I stick them into albums wherever there is room, no matter what is on its other pages. That's why I found photos of Ben Thomas squeezed in between my high-school graduation pictures and those of the birth of the twins.

Ben. Until that moment I'd nearly forgotten

about him. Without his picture staring out at me, I'm not sure I would fully remember his face anymore. Odd, since I'd once been head-over-heels in love with him.

College football star, math whiz, lady charmer Ben. But the most marvelous thing about him was that out of the hundreds of women on campus, most of whom were actively chasing him, he'd been attracted to me. I made him laugh, he'd said. And we'd laughed a lot in the two years we'd been together. He was going to be a veterinarian and I, another whiz kid in mathematics, was going to somehow save the world through numbers.

Ben was a public figure in those days. Student government, homecoming king, quarterback—a golden boy, so to speak.

It had been blissful for a time, that relationship of ours. I'd ordered a subscription to *Bride's Magazine* and started wandering through the china section of large department stores looking for the perfect pattern. Sometimes I'd even swing through the bridal department just, of course, to keep up on the fashions. Ben caught me a time or two and didn't protest, which, in my mind, sealed the deal. A June wedding, a starter house, a white picket fence and a dog—I had it planned perfectly. Unfortunately Ben changed the plans midstream without letting me know.

I sat back and recalled the fateful conversation that thrust my little fantasy into the harsh spotlight of reality.

"Suze, we've got to talk." Ben had looked more somber than usual and probably more handsome.

"Can it wait until after dinner? I've got a project to finish up."

"No. We need to talk now."

Never having heard that particular tone in his voice, I agreed immediately and followed him to a park bench on one of the large expanses of grass between buildings on campus.

"What's up?"

Ben looked at me with such a miserable expression on his face that he worried me.

"What's wrong? Something with one of your family?"

"No, nothing like that."

He'd called this meeting. Why wasn't he getting on with it?

"Suze, some of the guys have been...They think it's a big joke but...I know I'm probably wrong to feel this way but..."

"What are you talking about? And how is it you are supposed to feel?"

"I'm supposed to not care!"

I was completely confused. I put my hand on his arm but he pulled it away. "Don't do that, Suze. It's difficult enough already."

"Do what? Touch you?" A shudder of fear went through me, a foretaste of what was to come.

"I think you are probably the prettiest, funniest, most compassionate woman on this campus, Suze. Probably in this state or even the country," Ben rambled, "but I just can't help it. It makes me uncomfortable. Really uncomfortable. And with the guys ribbing me all the time, I've found it's something I don't think I can handle right now."

"What on earth are you talking about?" There was a dullness in Ben's pale blue eyes that I'd never seen there before and my senses had gone to high alert.

"A bunch of guys I know date girls in your dormitory. They talk about the crazy things you do in your sleep."

"That's no big deal. Everyone knows me by now. It's not as if I can help it, you know."

"Are you sure?" His expression brightened. "Take pills or something?"

I shook my head vigorously. "I tried that in high school. My parents made doctors run a gazillion tests on me, which proved nothing. All the meds did was make me disoriented and sleepy all day in class. I'd finally be waking up about the time I was supposed to take another one so I could go back to sleep."

"So you'll be like this for the rest of your life?"

"I suppose so. I'm not happy about it, if that's what you mean, but I'll get along." I glanced at him from beneath lowered lashes. "*We'll* get along."

He paled. "I'm not sure I want to get along with that, Suze."

At first I wasn't sure what he was saying. It was my problem, after all, not his.

But he'd made it his problem. "It's embarrassing, you know?"

"Better than anyone," I replied, not liking the way the conversation was going.

"I know I'm just a college kid right now, but I've got plans…aspirations. You know, goals."

"What does that have to do with anything, especially my sleepwalking?"

"I know we haven't discussed it much, Suze, but I've been thinking a lot about it lately. Maybe I don't want to go to veterinary school after all. My uncle is a state senator and he's been talking to me about going into politics."

While I'd been building and decorating my dream home, he'd decided to go into *politics?* I can still remember thinking that this was a far worse nightmare than any I'd had while I was asleep.

"My uncle says that I'll have to work hard to keep a good reputation if I plan to be a politician. He says I don't want to do anything that an opponent could use against me in an election."

So?

"I know it's not your fault but what you do *is* pretty weird. I don't think I can risk it. What if you jump in a car and run somebody over? How would that look?"

"You're dumping me because I sleepwalk?" I burst out laughing at the ridiculousness of it. Then I really looked at the expression on his face. "You're serious!"

"I'm sorry, Suze, but it's my life we're talking about. I can't take any chances, if you know what I mean…."

No, I didn't know. Not then and not now. All I'd known was that I was risky to care about because I might embarrass someone who tried to love me.

I stared hard at Ben's photo again and noticed, now that I was so far from the heady blush of love, that his chin was weak and his eyes, even in a photo, were averted.

It was another case of being fortunate to have

escaped. Ben now runs his father's machine shop in rural North Dakota, has six children and, according to Darla who still keeps track of him, has a string of failed political attempts including for Congress, state senate and mayor of a town of nine hundred people.

Yes, indeed, it's a good thing Ben got rid of me.

"Hey, Suze, it's Charley."

A thick knot tightened in my stomach. I've been waiting for his call—and dreading it.

He sounded terribly cheerful, something I wasn't after my sleepless night. It made me angry that Ben had the power to keep me awake even now. Of course, it wasn't really Ben that was troubling me. It was the legacy of hurt and self-doubt he'd left me with. I knew his excuses were feeble and ridiculous but how they'd made me feel had, through the years, stuck with me like glue.

"Chipper's new owner will be there about 7:00 p.m. to pick him up. Apparently she didn't come any sooner because she wanted to go on a dog-shopping extravaganza first. She read me her list—bed, bones, collars, jacket and booties, treats, customized water and food dishes and who knows what else. She's also ordered a dog house made to match her furniture so that if he needs privacy he has somewhere to go."

"She's not going to dress him in those outfits they sell, is she? I'd hate to see Chipper dressed up like Tinkerbelle and come to my door trick-or-treating at Halloween."

"I thought you'd be happy to know what a good home he's getting. This dog has landed in the lap of luxury."

"It's just that I'll miss him on *my* lap."

"I know," Charley said sympathetically, "but now, thanks to you, another animal has a second chance at life."

"I told you, I'm not taking another one for a while so don't bother bringing it over. I've got my hands full. Having my nephews in the house is equal to providing foster care for a dozen ferrets, sixteen kittens and a rhinoceros."

He didn't even tell me he thought I was exaggerating. He knows my nephews.

"Are you sure? Chester is going to need an experienced foster parent and you're my best."

"Flattery will get you nowhere, Charley. I just can't."

* * *

At 8:00 p.m., after Chipper's new owner had come to pick him up, I began to rethink my decision.

I had to be happy for the little dog. *Mama*, as his new owner prefers to be referred to when speaking of her budding relationship with Chipper, popped a rhinestone dog collar around his furry neck, fed him treat after treat from the pocket of her Donna Karan coat and cooed over him as if she'd just given birth. No, Chipper will do fine. I'm the one who's lonesome.

But how can one be lonesome when one has two darling rascally boys to keep her company?

They are *too* much company, actually. Nonstop, indefatigable, ridiculously enthusiastic company. He'd been gone less than an hour and I already wanted to sit serenely on the couch with Chipper, pet his fur and feel his little body relax against mine.

I almost reached for the phone to call Charley and ask him that if he had something less difficult than this needy Chester he kept talking about, but it rang before I could pick it up.

"Suze? Hi. You go it on the first ring. I didn't expect that." It was David. Even over the phone his voice is splendid.

"I'm glad you called. You just saved me from doing something very foolish."

"And that is?"

"I handed Chipper over to his new owner today."

"The little-three legged dog?"

David probably thought I should be happy to get rid of such a yippy, snippy creature.

"Yes. It's the hardest part about fostering animals. I always fall in love with them." Then I recalled Chipper leaving my house wrapped in a cashmere throw and having sweet nothings whispered in his ear and added, "But he's going to have it much better than he had it here. Designer dog food and everything."

"So what's wrong? Sounds like a great gig for Chipper."

"I'm lonely, that's all. If you hadn't called I might have picked up the phone and called Charley. He runs the rescue site and he says he has a new animal for me. I'm taking a couple months off while the boys are here and if I'd followed my impulse I would have regretted it later."

"So glad I could help." He paused before adding, "But I'm sorry you're lonely. Is there something I can do about that?"

There was definitely a lot he could do for me, but I didn't have time for a new relationship as long as the twins had me wrapped up 24/7.

"I don't think…"

"How about dinner? I'll be only a few blocks from your house tomorrow. I'll pick you up and bring you home again."

"I have the boys."

"Did your sister leave you a list of babysitters?"

Oh, he's a smart one, this Dr. David.

"A short one. Not many people come back to Mickey and Jeff's place twice."

"See if you can get someone to come for a few hours. We won't make it late. Besides, I hear in your voice that you could use a break."

Oh, boy, how could I!

"Have the sitter there by six forty-five. I'll pick you up at seven."

How could I resist?

"I'll have to call you if I can't coerce someone into watching the boys."

"You'll find someone. I already know that about you. If you want to do something, you get it done. And if you *don't* want to do it, nothing can convince you otherwise."

Was he referring to an admirable if tenacious quality in my personality? Or my stubbornness about not letting him play with my brain, give me an electrode helmet and watch me through a one-way window while I sleep?

Chapter Twelve

I backed out the door to my house just as David pulled into the driveway. He got out of the car, opened the passenger door and strolled up the walk, smiling.

Immediately I put a finger to my lips to signal him that he was not to make a sound. The baby-sitter, a mature woman who should have known better than to agree to come to my house, was in the kitchen with the twins. She'd engaged them with the offer of some very sloppy finger-painting if they didn't cause an uproar when I left. Their promises always have time limits and I only had about two minutes to get out of the way.

"Hurry, jump in the car. Let's go!"

We were turning the corner when I glanced back and saw my front door fly open. Tommy stood in the doorway scanning the street. Terry, no doubt, had the sitter, a woman who had raised nine children, occupied in the kitchen.

"That was close." I sank down in the lush leather of his car seat. "I almost didn't make it out."

"What might have happened if we'd been seen?"

"Who knows? Maybe nothing, maybe everything. The boys like it when I go out and have fun. They just want to come with me."

"Tonight is yours, Suze. Your wish is my command."

My wish was that I didn't have a barrelful of sleep disorders, I hadn't met David under such bizarre circumstances and that he'd plucked me out of a roomful of beauties as the love of his life, not picked me up off a hotel-room floor while I was gnawing ice cubes and begging for heavenly help. I also wished he'd stay interested in me until my responsibilities with the twins were done so I could rest and stop looking like a sleep-deprived prisoner. It just wasn't going to happen.

Still, I had this perfect late spring evening and I planned to enjoy it.

"What are my options?"

"What do you like? Baseball, dinner and

theater at the Guthrie, the zoo, the IMAX, the conservatory…"

"A picnic at Minnehaha Falls. It's a warm, beautiful evening." It was a test. Not just anyone can come up with a picnic on a moment's notice. Of course, I had underestimated David.

We stopped at a strip mall where David got out and went into a store, then came out with a large wicker basket outfitted with plates, forks and glasses.

"Next stop, the market. Tell me, what do you like to eat?"

"Picnic food." I was enjoying this.

At the market we found roasted chicken; potato, fruit and pasta salads; olives; croissants, watermelon and a half-dozen pastries. Before I knew it, we were sitting on the rocks near the falls watching the churning water and feeling the spray on our faces.

After we ate, David lay on a blanket he'd brought from the trunk of his car and I sat at his side, my arms wrapped around my knees, my face to the sky.

"What were you like as a child, David? I keep imagining you in a tiny suit reading encyclopedias."

His hearty laughter enveloped me. "I can

assure you that I didn't own a suit until junior high. I did, however, like pants with large pockets. With all the stones, sticks, frogs and lizards in the world, one can never have too many pockets, you know."

We talked idly and watched the couples who came to the falls. A wedding party moved into view, the bride in a painfully white gown embellished with bows and a groom who looked as if he was not old enough to drive.

When did weddings become competitions to see who could fit the most bridesmaids around an altar? The couple was trailed by nine women in pale blue dresses. The unfortunate dresses either made their wearers look pencil thin or like lumpy bags of marbles. Lagging even farther behind was a cluster of groomsmen who looked like a clutch of unhappy penguins.

Silently we watched them posing for photos with the falls in the background.

The thing that stood out above all else, at least in my mind, was the comfortable, easy relationship between the bride and groom. It was obvious that most of the time the gaggle of people with them and the curious passersby were invisible to them.

A verse from Proverbs popped into my mind. *The man who finds a wife finds a treasure and receives favor from the Lord.* This young man had obviously found his silver and gold.

I had never been Ben's treasure, nor he mine. We would have had a life of emotional poverty together.

I don't know why I asked the question but it spilled out of my mouth before I had time to filter it. "David, are you easily embarrassed?"

I shouldn't have looked at those old photos of Ben last night.

His handsome face was blank, as if he didn't understand the question.

"Have you ever been ashamed of someone close to you?"

"Embarrassed about what?" He looked genuinely puzzled.

"Oh, I don't know," I mumbled vaguely. "Insanity in the family, criminals, sleepwalkers…"

He burst out laughing. "Insanity, crime and sleepwalking? You're talking apples and oranges here, Suze. What's more, we love people for what they are. We don't have to like what they do but that doesn't mean we can't love them." He studied me intently. "I sense a hidden agenda here."

I jumped to my feet and held out my hands to him. "I have a sudden urge to see a movie."

When he hesitated, I added, "You promised, you know."

I didn't breathe a sigh of relief until we were settled in our theater seats, cloaked in darkness and burdened with popcorn and soda enough to feed a football team. I was too transparent. David seemed to see right through me. Still, it's comforting to know that he's not as judgmental as my youthful boyfriend had been.

Somehow between the previews and the movie's conclusion, David's hand had found mine in the bottom of the popcorn tub and wouldn't let go. I can't say I fought it either. We were still happily clinging to each other as we left the theater.

To my surprise and delight, the babysitter said she had actually enjoyed the experience and yes, she would come again. For a price.

"They're more work than I thought," the woman said. "I had to catch each one and put them to bed several times before they realized I meant business. And baths...Well, you'll have to get all new toiletries. They'd made a concoction with the lot of them in the bathtub before I caught them. You'll need milk and eggs, too. I couldn't get the shelf back on the inside of your refrigerator door after Terry tried to ride on it and pulled it off."

I held my hand in the air to stop the torrent of information. I didn't care. The boys were alive, the house had not burned down and the woman, for only twice what I'd offered her tonight, would return. A cabinet full of shampoo and perfume and the cost of a repairman was a small price to pay for a night of freedom.

I wandered around after she left, closing drapes and turning off lights.

The house was too quiet. Hammie was asleep on the wheel but even if he'd been awake, I wouldn't have heard him now that David had repaired it. Chipper was not there to greet me at the door with his high-pitched yap. And after an evening with David, the night seemed surprisingly empty without him.

Chapter Thirteen

Charley caught me as I was about to leave my office the next afternoon.

"What are you doing here?"

"Thought I'd come by and take you out for a quick cup of coffee before you pick up the dynamic duo." He stared at me. "You look horrible, what's up?"

"I'm not sleeping well, that's all. I thought I'd get a nap before I got the boys."

"Chamomile tea, then. I need to talk to you."

I stared at him. Charley and I have known each other forever but I'd never had him come to find me at the office. "Is something wrong?"

"Yes and no." He pointed to a java joint. "How about there?"

"It must be serious, for you to drive here to talk to me."

"Let me get you some tea, then we'll talk."

I had nervous butterflies in my stomach by the time he returned with the beverages. "Don't keep me in suspense any longer," I ordered. "Why are you here? Is it good news or bad?"

"A little of both, I think. The rescue is doing really well these past weeks. We've placed a lot of animals and as a result have room to take in others."

"So? That doesn't warrant a trip into downtown Minneapolis to tell me."

He looked deep into his mug. "We placed the last of our current batch of foster pets today."

"Really? That's wonderful!"

"I placed Hammie, Suze. I know you've had him a long, long time but the deal with the rescue is that when a good home comes up…"

Hammie? He'd come to me half-dead, emaciated, his fur matted, a pitiful little thing indistinguishable from a large mouse. Today he is fat and glossy. Hammie loves me. Sometimes at night, before the twins came to stay, Hammie and I sat on the couch and watched old movies. He'd curl up on my chest, put his stubby little nose in the curve of my neck and fall asleep. Hamsters snore. I've heard it with my own ears.

"I thought that after all this time…Hamsters

are a dime a dozen, Charley, why can't they get another one?"

"It's a couple with a child terrified of animals. The only critter the child has ever showed any interest in is a hamster in a pet-store window. The world's tamest hamster is Hammie."

"I could tame another one for her," I offered, know-ing already that Hammie would go where he was needed.

"They promised that if it didn't work out, they'd bring him right back, but frankly, I know this child's dad and he'll take excellent care of him."

"Hammie and Chipper in the same week?"

"The bad news is that they're gone. The good news is that now you have room for somebody else."

"After the twins leave, I'll take a couple, but for now…" I had an unexpected catch in my throat. "You slimeball, you know I can't get along without pets in my house."

Charley grinned at me. "I've got Chester in my car if you'd like to take him right now. I'll bring him over and pick up the hamster. What do you think?"

"You're a low-down, tricky…"

"Effective administrator. Have you any idea

how many impossible-to-place animals we've found homes for because of you?"

It's true. I'm a lifesaver—literally.

"Give me the lecture later, Charley." A tiny alarm bell went off in my head. "Why is it that you're so eager to foist this cat off on me in particular? Lots of the volunteers enjoy taking the cats."

An odd expression flitted across his face and was gone. "This cat has your name on it, Suze, that's all."

"Then I don't want it. I'm not taking any more pets unless I get to say when—and *if*— they are placed. From now on, I get first say. And if I want to keep them all, I don't want to hear another word about it."

"All of them?"

"Maybe I exaggerated a little for effect. I feel obligated to give up Hammie because he's already been promised. But from now on…"

"It's your own fault, you know. We've never had an animal you've fostered not become fit for adoption. You should have thirty acres of land and a dozen barns and spend all your time and energy rescuing misfits," Charley said. He looked out at the skyscrapers. "I don't know how the people in those things stand it. At least you and I have yards."

"Some of them love it," I responded softly.

"Nobody who wants a lot of animals around," Charley retorted.

Like David Grant? I wondered.

"Go get your car," Charley ordered.

"I have to pick up the twins."

"I'll be right behind you."

When we got to the house, the lights were already on. Inside, I could smell something delicious cooking in the kitchen. There was a small fire in the fireplace; the lights were dim and soothing. The toys had been picked up. An angel had landed here while I was gone.

At that moment, Darla came bustling out of the kitchen in one of my aprons. Don't Bother Kissing the Cook, Just Do the Dishes it said.

"There you are. I wanted to surprise you." Her voice trailed away and she stared not at me but over my left shoulder where Charley stood.

I didn't blame her for gawking. Most people do. Charley's Mohawk was highlighted with pink today and he had a safety pin through his eyebrow. It seemed all the more alarming considering he was wearing a finely tailored three-piece suit. The contradictory messages he sent confused everyone. Poor Darla couldn't be expected to understand.

Before Darla could speak, Charley stepped

forward and held out his hand. "Charles Cousins, I run the pet rescue that Suze works for. You must be Darla. Suze has told me a lot about you. I'm delighted to meet you."

Darla gave me a panicked look.

"Charley is one of my best buddies," I explained. "When he's not running the rescue he is an actor."

Her shoulders relaxed. He's in costume, I knew she was thinking. I didn't dissuade her.

"I'm pleased to meet you, too." She beamed at him. "Any friend of Suze's is a friend of mine."

As they shook hands, it evoked the image of a lit Fourth of July sparkler. Hot, bright luminosity seemed to pass between them and they both drew quickly back as if they'd been stung. Darla's blue eyes were wide and Charley's usual blasé demeanor vanished. They stammered and nodded and pretended that they hadn't felt what I had so clearly observed.

Darla and Charley? The beauty and the beast?

I really haven't been getting enough sleep.

They stumbled awkwardly around each other after that and I was almost relieved to have Charley carry Hammie and his cage out of the house.

As soon as he was outside, Darla was in my face. "Who *is* that?"

"Just my buddy. Why?" I acted innocent.

"He's so…so…strange."

"And wonderful?"

"What gives with the hairdo? For a part in a play, I hope."

"In Charley's own play—his life. He's currently starring as a parrot. He likes to keep people off guard. He's an old teddy bear and I think it's his way of being 'tough.' He'd give anyone the shirt off his back—and has a number of times. When the shirt is shredded and decorated with safety pins and painted with his personal rendition of baby dragons, fewer people ask for it."

"He's weird, in other words." Darla sounded disappointed.

"Not at all. He's creative."

"A synonym for *weird*."

"People, including you and my family, call me creative. Should I take that to mean you think *I'm* weird?"

"If the shoe fits, wear it," Darla muttered. Then she gave me a lopsided smile. "You aren't weird. Point taken. Don't judge a book by its cover."

"Or a man by his Mohawk."

Just then Charley returned with a large cardboard box lined with a snagged and tattered blanket. The edge of the blanket was draped back over the top of the box, concealing the contents.

"Charley, I've been thinking...."

He pulled back the corner of the blanket and revealed the box's contents.

Inside was an emaciated cat that looked no larger than an eight- or ten-week-old kitten. His fur was matted, his paws raw and bloody and he trembled so that the box quivered in Charley's arms. But his eyes! They were the size of large marbles in the scrawny face, blue as the sky on a sunny day during a Minnesota winter. They were old, wise eyes that looked as if they'd seen too much in his short life.

"What happened to him?" Darla gasped.

"I don't even care to guess," Charley said grimly. "Someone found him and was going to have him put down but then decided to bring him to our shelter. He's going to take a lot of time and attention and someone with a lot of patience. He's terrified of everyone and everything. Suze is the only choice. Everybody else has their quota and no one is as good with the really struggling ones as she is."

He turned to me and I saw that soft underbelly of his he's always trying to hide. "You will take him, won't you?"

"Oh, Charley, this cat is going to be too much work. I've got the twins." *And I'm only sleeping four hours a day.* "I just can't."

"Of course you can. I'm here," Darla said, bustling across the room to where Charley and I stood. "I'll help with the boys while you care for—" she peered into the tattered box "—that."

I was still processing how all this had come about when Charley left. The pathetic creature in the box and I locked eyes and stared at each other. Last chances, that was what this was all about, and I was his. This cat had used up all his nine lives and about twenty-five he'd borrowed from others.

"What did you do that for?" I demanded when Darla returned from the kitchen where she'd checked on both dinner and the boys.

"Look at that thing. If you didn't take it, you know what would happen to it."

"I thought you didn't like cats much. Since when did you get a feeling for saving the earth and everything in it?"

Darla sat down and gazed at me. The expression on her features was remarkably thoughtful and serious. "Remember the time we were talking about the idea of stewardship and what it means for Christians?"

"Sure. You said it meant tithing and making sandwiches and salads for funerals."

"And you said it meant taking seriously the idea of tending to all of God's creatures, that the earth was our responsibility and we needed to treat it as such."

"So? Not everyone agrees with me."

"I think I do. I'm beginning to see that tiny acts of goodness are as important as large, blatant acts. They add up. I can't donate a million dollars to a favorite charity, but I can go to a soup kitchen and help out, I can make a Christmas basket for a family so their kids can have toys, and I can be kind to something or someone that everyone else has overlooked and I can be sure that I don't waste resources just because they are there. Let's just say that I've begun to look at what you do as a form of stewardship. Being kind with no chance of reward or thanks takes practice." She looked at the flea-ridden mess in the box. "This is good practice."

My heart felt as though it might burst. "So you *do* listen to me once in a while. I'm never quite sure."

"*Once* in a while." Then she twinkled at me with her baby blues. "And maybe that Charley guy will stop by and check on this cat once in a while. I'd like to observe him—for purely scientific reasons, of course."

Scientific, right—the science of the heart.

Chapter Fourteen

Wouldn't you know it? The night Darla finally arrived—the night I was to begin to catch up on all that lost sleep—was the night Chester came into my life.

I've never lost much sleep over a man—except for David the other night—but a cat...that's a different story entirely.

Chester refused to move from the corner of his box, as if the tattered rags of his little nest were all he had for protection. That part was probably true, or had been until now, but Chester had no idea he'd landed in the lap of luxury so he clung to the tattered bit of safety he knew.

I set up a litter box, water and dry food in my laundry room, turned on a night-light, closed the door and hoped he'd dare venture out to explore his new surroundings once the house was quiet. Then I padded happily to my bed. No more infomercials, no more struggling to stay awake so that I didn't pack up the boys and haul them off to an amusement park at 3:00 a.m. No more bone-crushing fatigue at work... But I hadn't figured on Chester in my equation.

He started yowling the moment my head hit the pillow. I shot straight up, heart pounding, already half-asleep and disoriented. I grabbed my robe and headed for the laundry room. Two accusing feral eyes gleamed out at me from the cardboard box. He'd been out to use the litter box and eat the food down to the last bit. The water was gone, too. It appeared that he'd had his first good meal in ages. Unfortunately it had given him strength to do what he'd wanted to do all along—complain about the pathetic nature of his life, the injustice of brutal or neglectful owners and, apparently, the state of world politics. He had much to complain about and did so all night long.

Darla found me in the morning, sprawled across the laundry-room floor, my arm over Chester's box.

"Sleepwalking?" She'd squatted down beside me and opened one of my eyelids, much as the twins do.

"No. Unfortunately I did this intentionally. Did you get any sleep at all?"

"What do you mean? I slept like a baby… and so did the babies."

"You didn't hear this creature howling at the moon? I've been in here all night. The only time he doesn't yowl is when I'm with him." I rolled over and groaned. Sleeping on the floor might be okay when you're five or six, but those ages are long gone in my rearview mirror. I felt as if I'd been rolled over by a street sweeper.

"Don't tell me you didn't sleep last night either! Suze, this is ridiculous. Next thing you know, your friends and family will be checking you into a sanitarium for the sleep deprived and insane. You should have let me help you."

"You mean you would have slept on my laundry-room floor with a feral cat with emotional issues while I dozed in my bed?"

"When you put it that way, no. If I did, you'd have to put *me* in the sanitarium, too."

My antennae, which were also sleep-deprived, finally kicked into functioning mode. "Darla, where are the boys?"

"They're fine. I left them in the bathroom brushing their teeth."

I stared at her in horror. "You left them? In a room with a temptation larger than Eve's apple?"

"What might that be?" Darla, the uninitiated, looked truly puzzled. "You've got a lock on your medicine cabinet."

"The toilet, of course! Do you know how many times Mickey and Jeff have had to have a plumber…"

We both raced into the bathroom just in time to see Tommy pour my favorite perfume into the bowl, anointing my new red bra, which was now whirling and twirling its way into the depths of the Twin Cities sewer system.

Darla made me take the day off.

Fortunately Chester was as exhausted from last night as me and we both got several hours of solid sleep. And we both woke up crying.

His wails were silenced by more food. I think I could have fed an entire army of cats with the amount he was eating but I had no idea how long the poor thing had been neglected and gone hungry.

I, however, woke up with tears in my eyes and nothing, not even a vanilla éclair with chocolate frosting could dry me up. In the beautiful and scarce silence of my home, I, still exhausted and depressed, bawled like a baby.

By afternoon things were looking better. I can feel sorry for myself for a little while, but

I don't let it go on too long. In the scheme of things my tribulations are not problems at all but miniscule blips on life's radar. When I feel a pity party coming on, I start saying thanks to God for all the things that are still *right* with me—a home, food, job, friends, family, to name a few—and the fact that a cat kept me awake all night and I'm not to be trusted in strange hotel rooms—seems pretty manageable.

I was also grateful that Terry and Tommy were at their sitter's place.

I was still in gratitude mode when the doorbell rang. Although I hadn't yet combed my hair or washed my face and I was still holding Chester who had finally decided that anyone nuts enough to stay up all night with him couldn't be all bad. He'd snuggled into my arms like a twiggy bag of pickup sticks and fallen asleep against my chest, my arm tucked beneath his bony little hips. His warm if withered body was as much a comfort to me as mine was to him. I had stayed in my faded sleep pants and bleach-spotted Old Navy sweatshirt all day, holding him. Now I lamented the fact I had to answer the door.

I flung it open, matted and filthy Chester still sleeping, attached to me as if by Velcro. I'd assumed the mailman would be standing on my porch with a package.

It was a package all right, a hunky and handsome package in gray trousers, a camel-colored cashmere coat and white shirt.

"David? What are you doing here?" Chester and I together must have made quite a picture, akin to refugees in a war-ravaged Third World country.

"I called your office to talk to you and your friend Darla came on the line. She said you'd had a bad night—several nights, actually—and that I should come right over and check on you." He looked me over and the concern on his face deepened. "You do look pretty bad. And what's that ratty fur thing you're holding?"

Chester took that moment to open one eye.

David stepped back. "It's alive!"

"Barely. This is Chester, my new foster cat. He's had a hard life."

"Obviously." David looked doubtful. "He looks disease ridden."

"Charley had him checked out. He's starved, abused and mishandled, has emotional issues and is terrified, but the vet says, miracle of miracles, he's healthy."

I paused to regroup and consider what David had said. "And what do you mean 'I look pretty bad' and what business is it of Darla's whether or not I slept last night?"

"*Bad* is a relative term, Suze. You're still beautiful. You just aren't…er…stunning." He looked miserable, and perversely I felt pleased.

"Stunned more than stunning, is that what you mean?" I sighed and stepped aside so he could come in.

"I thought I'd sleep last night since Darla was here and I wouldn't have to worry so much about the boys, but the cat howled all night. I had to sleep with my arm over him in order for him to be quiet. Let's just say it's not comfortable on my laundry-room floor."

"Have you considered that you may take your job too seriously? Aren't there rules about letting stray animals overtake you and your home?"

Nothing he said could have ruffled my feathers more. "What do you mean?"

He appeared to realize that he'd gone too far but didn't know how to back out. "If any stray cat landed on your doorstep, would you bring it inside and let it take over your home?"

"Of course not. I make it a policy not to fall in love with strays. I make sure I don't have them inside and I certainly don't make a fuss over them. If I were to pet and cuddle them too much we'd bond."

David's eyebrow lifted quizzically.

"Well, I'd bond a little. Maybe I'd play with it or pick it up, but is that so bad?"

"But you'd leave it outside, correct?"

I scuffed the toe of my slipper against the floor. "I make exceptions. I've let cats and other critters stay in my laundry room. It's pleasant in there and there's a nice big window so they can laze in the sun."

"So you never let them inside and fuss with them unless it's an exception?"

"Isn't that what I just said?"

"How many exceptions have you had?"

"They've all been exceptions so far, but that doesn't mean anything. I've still got rules."

"Well, at least they can't get any farther than the laundry room." He studied my face with benign amusement. "Can they?"

"If they're in the house, they aren't allowed on the furniture. Okay, some of the furniture, but not the good things. And they certainly can't sharpen their claws on anything! That's what I bought the scratching post for."

"You bought a scratching post for stray cats?"

"Well, yes…"

"I have to congratulate you, Suze. You certainly have managed to take control of the animals in your life."

Why does he look entertained and amused by me so much of the time?

I certainly don't feel all that fascinating. In fact, I feel like dropping onto the couch and sleeping for days.

Much to my horror, tears came to my eyes.

His expression changed immediately, and he was at my side.

"What is it?"

"I'm just so tired, David. Please forgive me. I'll be fine after…"

He took me by the shoulders and I realized how much taller he was than me. And strong. And how good he smelled close up. "You are not okay. You haven't been 'okay' for a long time as far as I can tell. What you are is stubborn, obstinate and mulish."

Mulish? At least that was animal related. I could handle that.

But David wasn't finished. "For some reason you've convinced yourself that there's no help for you and you won't hear any differently. I can't force you to do anything but I can beg you, as a friend, to please let someone try to help you."

He stepped back and I missed the heat of his hands on my shoulders. "Let me recommend a man at my clinic. There would be no conflict of interest between us and I could support you as a friend, not as a physician. The man I'm suggesting is top notch. What do you have to lose?" He eyed me, barefoot, rumpled and hanging on to a cat that looked more like a furry bird's nest than an animal.

"From your point of view, not much, I'm sure." I felt tears at the back of my throat and hated myself for it.

"And from yours?" His gaze was so intent that it seemed to hook my soul and pull the words up through my throat and out into the open.

"Hope, David, hope. Every time I've gone through these tests, I have had hope. If I do it again and it fails again, do you have any idea of how I'll feel?"

"If you don't try then you can't fail, you mean?"

"Skewed, I know, but silly as it sounds, it is true." I paused. "If I do this and am disappointed again, there's nowhere else to go. I'm afraid I'll quit fighting it, David. I can't do that. I have to keep trying."

He gathered me and Chester into his arms. Chester gave a grunt of disapproval at being made into a cat sandwich, but he didn't try to get away. "Let me walk this with you, Suze. I won't let you give up hope or quit trying.

Taking another stab at the tests, trying the advances we've made, it's not a prescription for failure. It's just another shot at the same target, that's all. If it doesn't work, you still have your sleep disorder. And if it does…"

I don't know why I agreed. It wasn't because I had any hope whatsoever of a solution to my problem. Instead, it was probably how David's cologne drifted into my nostrils and how his arms felt around me. And how he said he'd walk the path with me this time. At the moment, I would have done almost anything for an opportunity to add that to my life.

"Coffee?" I asked. "I'll make you some." Then I paused, feeling puzzled. "And since when does a big-shot neurologist, head of a sleep clinic, VIP doctor make house calls?"

"I'd love some coffee but I want you to get the stuff—decaf, too—out of your house until we figure out what's going on with you." He smiled slightly. "And this doctor makes house calls because the six-hour meeting he had scheduled today got called off." He shrugged, grinned and spread his hands, palm up, in a happy-but-helpless gesture.

"So everything was moved to tomorrow and I've been a doctor long enough to know that if a free day comes to jump on it. I also know that if I go to the clinic to see how things are going, I'll never get out again. I look at this as a test. I want to see if the staff can fly without me."

After returning Chester to his ragged hidey-hole, I spooned coffee into the filter basket and took cream out of the refrigerator. Fortunately I had made muffins yesterday so I had something to feed David. Unfortunately they were my grandmother's recipe and something of an acquired taste. My grandmother believes in fiber. And I mean *fiber*.

When my grandmother talks about having "smooth sailing" in her life, she means she's got all the fiber she needs in her system. It appears her roughage needs are high because she puts it in everything from soup in the form of unpeeled, undercooked vegetables to mashed potatoes cooked skin-on.

Sometimes Darla complains that our family eats like goats and squirrels, neither of which is known for having a smooth, creamy diet.

I handed David a plate and a mug of coffee, then transferred some muffins—small but weighing about a half pound each—to another plate. He took one and hefted it as if it might a bag of money. "A substantial muffin," he commented cautiously.

"Heavy ingredients," I said, taking one

myself and breaking it open. "Carrots, pecans, pineapple, coconut, wheat flour, flaxseed, prunes, a hint of oatmeal…"

"An organic paradise," he concluded.

"I apologize in advance for whatever this might do to your digestive system but they're good for you."

He looked at me studiously. "I have to admit, Suze, you are by far the most exceptional woman I have ever met."

"Who? Little ol' me? Why thank you, sir, but I bet you say that to all the girls." I fluttered my eyelashes outrageously and handed him the butter—my little rebellion against Granny's good food rules.

"Only the ones who appear to have starving animals glued to their chests and proudly serve muffins made out of the same material as bowling balls."

"You sweet talker, you. I can see you have exotic tastes."

David was easy to tease. The fan of fine laugh lines near his eyes made him approachable. For a man with so much education and importance, he didn't take himself too seriously. If I were to describe him with only one word—and not the obvious ones like *handsome, hunky, gorgeous* or *adorable*—the word

I'd choose is *compassionate*. A close runner-up would be *kind*.

He not only didn't hate Granny's health muffins, he actually liked them. I had to stop him after the first one, however. I never know how the muffins will affect people. Darla had a stomachache for two days after her first one. Her stomach had never had to work so hard to digest anything in its life except maybe that pile of peanut shells someone had dared her to eat at a sorority house party.

Just as I was telling David this story, the doorbell rang.

Chester, startled by the sound, began to yowl, so I picked him up before going to answer the door.

"I'm going to have to change clothes," I muttered. Soon everyone would think I always dress myself out of the garbage can at Goodwill.

Before I could get to the door, Darla bolted into the kitchen with the twins in tow.

She looked wild-eyed. "Someone called to have me bring the boys home—something about backed-up plumbing at day care."

Where have I heard that before? Mickey's on a first-name basis with her plumber. The boys appeared dopey and immediately went to their room and fell asleep. Tired, perhaps, from botching up someone's pipes?

Darla peered at me. "Are you okay? I'm glad to have the opportunity to come to check on you. You were acting really weird this morning." She moved toward the coffeepot. "I honestly thought you'd passed out on the laundry-room floor... Oh, hello, David, so nice to see you."

"So you sent David on a rescue mission?"

"I was hoping he'd come but I didn't know for sure."

I turned to David. "Please send the invoice for this house call to Darla. Make it big. I want her to quit meddling in my life. I've talked to her about it but it doesn't help. Perhaps a ridiculously large bill for your services will wake her up."

"I couldn't, not in good conscience, at least not anymore. In one cup of coffee and one muffin in this house, I had the caloric equivalent of sixteen regular muffins and the caffeine punch of Rocky Balboa."

"It's decaffeinated."

"And as I've said before, I'd recommend you quit drinking it altogether."

I threw my hands in the air and Chester hung on for dear life. "I don't know which of you is worse!"

"Say it's me, please say it's me," Darla retorted cheerfully. "I want to be the one responsible for helping you to get over this malady you have."

"It's not a malady. It's just a little issue."

"Right. That's why I found you sleeping with your head in the cat's water dish, because of your little issue."

"I was not!" I protested but then stopped. "Was I?"

Darla turned to David triumphantly. "See?"

He nodded solemnly. "Point taken."

I was about to yell at them both but the doorbell rang again. Had someone hung a Welcome to Grand Central Station sign on my front door?

Chapter Fifteen

Charley, his Mohawk particularly bright and perky in hot-pink and turquoise, stood at the door staring at my chest and grinning.

I didn't take that in a bad way, especially since Chester was the one he was eyeing, as the cat clung to me like a tree frog.

"I see you two have bonded."

"Whatever," I said wearily. "He likes me in an approach-avoidance sort of way." I peeled the cat off my sweater and handed him to Charley. Chester meowed pitifully but curled up in his arms.

"Who is here?" Darla skidded to a stop in the doorway of the kitchen to stare at Charley.

He did make quite a sight in holey jeans, a high-necked black turtleneck, his suit coat, bright green sneakers and a collection of peace-symbol necklaces he must have lifted from an aging hippy. I hope he quits doing avant-garde theater soon. It's having a rather nasty effect on his dressing habits.

"I came to see how the cat is doing. Well, hello there." Charley locked eyes with Darla and forgot about Chester.

She was framed in the doorway looking like a gorgeous kewpie doll in a vibrant yellow business suit. Darla was a cute little parakeet to Charley's outlandish parrot.

Something weird was going on again; little electrical sparks seemed to be flowing back and forth between Charley and Darla like a mini force field. Charley's brown eyes were telepathically glued to Darla's and whatever was being transmitted between them must have been mighty interesting because neither seemed inclined to break the gaze.

Then Chester put a claw into Charley's chest. He yelped and danced around pulling at the matted furball, and Darla spun around and retreated to the kitchen like a frightened kitten herself.

"What was that about?" I demanded when Charley and Chester had settled their differences.

"A claw to the pectoral, that's what. It stung."

"Not that. Whatever was going on between you and my friend Darla. Shazam! Wow! Whee! That stuff."

"I make eye contact with a woman and you turn into Sherlock Holmes."

"That wasn't eye contact, Charley, it was a mind-meld."

"You need more sleep, Suze, you're imagining things."

For once I was sure that what was going on had nothing to do with my sleep deprivation, but I wasn't going to get any more out of Charley right now. Besides, I had Dr. Pillow in my kitchen and I was ignoring him. Bad form. Very bad form.

David was patiently waiting in the kitchen, his hands around a freshly poured mug of coffee and a suspicious eye on Darla, who was madly primping in the reflection of the toaster.

He raised one eyebrow when he saw Charley behind me but otherwise appeared unfazed by the dog and pony, er, rather… cat and clown… show being played out in my house.

If it hadn't been for David, the next few minutes might have been some of the longest of my life. He was the one who kept the conversation going while I brewed more coffee and tried to pretend that Darla's and Charley's brains hadn't frozen.

When Darla regained consciousness and realized that she needed to get back to work, Charley found an excuse to leave the house at the same time. I walked them to the door, and hoped that Darla wouldn't get a glimpse of the jalopy he drives. He's painted it with theater scenes—Shakespeare, Coward and even Andrew Lloyd Webber—but instead of painting human beings into the parts, he populated the stage with dogs and cats. There's a Persian kitten doing a soliloquy from *Hamlet*, a Doberman wearing the Phantom of the Opera's mask and cape, and a portrait of King Lear that looks suspiciously like his royal highness was part schnauzer.

I loped back to the kitchen and flung myself into a chair. "Welcome to my surreal life."

"Your waking hours do have the quality of a dream state," David acknowledged. "No wonder you can't tell when you're awake and when you are asleep."

"Is that your professional diagnosis?"

"No, just an observation. By the way, were there a lot of pheromones floating around this room just a few minutes ago?"

"Don't ask me to explain why. Darla and Charley are as unlikely a pair as exists. Darla, for all her fluffy looks, has a mind like a steel trap. She's as adept with numbers as she is with the English language. Her favorite class in college was calculus. Charley, on the other hand, was one of those theater people who dressed in black, could quote entire acts of plays, direct *Oklahoma!* but forget where he parked his car. How could a relationship like that flourish? They don't speak the same language. Could they trust each other when their worlds are so disparate?"

"When are you going to trust me, Suze?" David swirled the dregs of his coffee in the bottom of the mug and studied me with those disconcerting eyes of his. He's a bewildering combination of suave sophisticate in his appearance, extraordinary competence in his professional life and down-to-earth boyish practicality in his appeal. The portions are in just the right balance too. He's a very difficult package to resist.

I've known a lot of wonderful men, some of whom even asked me to marry them, but I've never really allowed myself to fall in love, not fully, not unconditionally. I suppose it's because I've never felt quite whole myself. In a sense, I'm damaged goods. What man wants to wake up in the middle of the night with me trying to put his shoes on or humming reveille at 3:00 a.m.?

I'd had this conversation with Darla not long ago.

"My sister Mickey has always told me she thinks I'm more interesting asleep than awake," I'd told her. "She means it as a joke, of course, but I've taken it to heart."

"You shouldn't let one person's flippant comment affect you so much." Darla had looked perturbed. "That's just mean of your sister."

"Oh, it wasn't just one person. My grand-mother's sister, my aunt Minnie, told me, 'What man is going to want a woman like you, Suze? You'd be far too much trouble.'"

At the time, that had really stung.

Logically I know I should ignore Aunt Minnie. She's known in the family for having the sensitivity of a camel's hide, the tact of a railroad spike, the diplomacy of a nuclear weapon and the compassion of a pack of wolves going in for the kill. *She's* the one who is too much trouble. She was engaged twelve times and is still single to this day, in her eighties. Twelve times her suitors ran off before the wedding, just after Minnie began to show her true self and the double-bladed sharpness of her tongue. That should tell me something. Still, her words hurt and, worse yet, they had stayed with me, just under the surface, appearing only when I thought it might be safe to fall in love.

Apparently I'm screwy when I'm awake as well as asleep, I'd concluded. It wasn't David that I didn't trust—the man is a poster boy for integrity and competence—I didn't trust me.

"It's complicated, David."

"I find 'complicated' to be far more interesting than banal and predictable."

He reached out and touched my hand. It was suddenly very clear that it was not just as a sleep specialist adviser that he wanted to be trusted.

How had that happened so rapidly? Of course, it had happened just as quickly for me. I could fall in love with this guy, head over heels and throw caution to the winds. But what would happen when we both came to our senses? When I accidentally pushed him out a window on the honeymoon, for example?

"We need to talk, Suze. I'm sure it's perfectly clear that I have two agendas. One is to find you a neurologist who can help you. The second is that I want to get to know you better. I'm not your doctor and I don't want to be. Maybe I want something more."

My knees began to tingle, a sure sign that I

was excited. When others get a "tingling feeling all over," I get it in my knees. More proof my circuitry is all botched up.

"Get a babysitter for tonight. Let me take you out for dinner. We'll talk, get to know each other. The twins will be fine for a few hours…."

The *twins!* I glanced at the clock. I hadn't heard from them since they'd lain down for their naps. A bad feeling settled in my stomach, the place I most feel fear.

"I forgot all about them!" I pushed away from the table and stood up.

"They're asleep." David looked puzzled. "Wouldn't you have heard them if they'd gotten up?"

"Oh, David, you are so naive. So pathetically, innocently naive. And totally inexperienced in the ways of the Terror Twins." With that, I shot off for the boys' bedroom. David was close behind.

It is absolutely amazing how much destruction can be done by round-tipped, blunt edged child's scissors and a box of crayons when in the hands of two masters.

The boys had retrieved—from the top shelf of the bedroom closet—the plastic shoe box of craft items I keep there for them. We often make birthday cards for family members so the boys can proudly present their own offerings when a celebration is taking place. There's nothing in the box that can hurt them—the finger paints are nontoxic as is the glitter glue and markers. It's what the things in the box could do to the rest of the room that horrified me.

"Wha ..," I heard David mutter behind me.

"I know. The twins' handiwork is something to behold the first time you see it. Frankly I'm still amazed at how much they can destroy in so little time and with so few tools."

"They're going to grow up to be plastic surgeons." David's voice was heavy with amazement.

"Or interior decorators."

Tommy and Terry had, in whatever time they'd been awake, not only found a way—involving a chair, a phonebook and a yardstick—to get down the craft items but also to meticulously glue my drapes together, pleat by pleat, from the floor upward as high as they could reach. Then they'd done trompe l'oeil along the bottom of the two largest walls.

The boys probably will be artists of some sort or in a profession that requires an artistic eye and skilled fingers—like cosmetic dentistry or, as David suggested, plastic surgery. They had actually managed a little theme in their artistry—a bold thread of red crayon running through jagged lightning bolts of green and black, and punctuated with bright yellow and orange suns with rays that reached from the bottom of the wall to over the twins' heads.

I groaned and sat down on the floor. Immediately both boys were at my side, stroking my cheeks and hair and saying, "We made it pretty for you!"

I looked up at David who, the scoundrel, tried to suppress a grin.

"You boys aren't supposed to draw on the walls. And what have you done to my drapes?"

Here it comes, I thought. Terry's eyes grew wide and welled with tears. Tommy's lower lip began to wobble tremulously. The next thing I'd hear was remorseful, penitent wails. The boys, though terrorists in the making, are deeply sensitive when anyone questions their good intentions.

I grabbed them by their Spider-man T-shirts and put them in front of me. "I know you wanted to do something pretty. You always do. But you can't be wrecking my house!"

"Mommy lets us," Terry observed, his remorse already vanished.

I looked up at David. "And the truth comes out."

"You're sure your mommy lets you?" I demanded, determined to get to the bottom of the cryptic statement. "What does she say when she 'lets' you do this?"

Tommy squirmed out of my grasp and, with a theatrical flair that would have thrilled Charley to death, did a swoon worthy of Sarah Bernhardt. He put the back of his wrist to his forehead, moaned histrionically and, whimpering, fell to the floor in a faint. Tommy opened one eye and gazed at me. "Like that."

I heard David choke back laughter and walk from the room. Tommy and Terry eyed me warily. I was not their mommy and not prone to fainting.

After I set them to work scrubbing the walls with two of the many crayon erasers I keep on hand, I returned to the kitchen where David was refilling his coffee cup. He was still grinning.

"How can you keep a straight face when those two do something like that? They're hilarious."

"It obviously is not your walls and drapes we're talking about."

Uproarious giggles came from the back room.

"Now what are they doing?"

"Cleaning. Fortunately they don't seem to

mind. As far as I can tell, they just need to be directed and busy." I scraped my glue-and-glitter decorated fingers through my hair. "Unfortunately, it takes a Ph.D. to keep them that way."

Much to my amazement, David put down his mug, strode across the room and put his warm, strong hands on my shoulders. "You have *got* to have dinner with me tonight."

"I feel like I've been dragged through a knothole in a toothpick. Why would you or anyone else want my company?"

"Suze, quite frankly, you become more captivating by the moment. Granted, you're particularly fascinating because of the way we met, but your house, your nephews, your animals… Let's just say you are an intriguing change…"

Mentally I filled in the blank for him: …*from the other women I know.*

"I like your approach to life." His dark gaze bored into mine.

I felt myself slipping under his spell. *Hang on, Suze, don't get your hopes up.*

Fortunately Chester chose that moment to morph into a watchdog and my guardian, and bolted out of nowhere to land hissing, claws extended, onto David's pant leg.

Chapter Sixteen

To his credit, David hardly screamed at all. Chester did, however, manage to snag a very pricey pair of trousers.

"I don't think your watch-cat wants you to go out with me."

The idea of being away from my house for the evening was very enticing.

"Let's see what I can do about a babysitter. I don't want to ask Darla. She's done enough." I picked up my handheld and dialed my parents' house. They'd had a weekend in Florida. They should be rested enough to handle it.

"I was just thinking about you," Mom said brightly when she answered the phone. "Your sister e-mailed me to ask how you were holding up. I wrote back, telling her that Dad and I would stop by tonight so that you could go out for a few hours. How does that sound?"

Wonderful, I thought. "Perfect. What time can you be here?"

She seemed a little taken aback at the swiftness with which I accepted, but promised to be at my house by seven. Mom and Dad tag-team the boys and manage pretty well. Mom gives the pair cookies for good behavior. Dad teaches them card games that Mickey would probably rather not have them know, but they play for toothpicks, not money so it seems shady but not outright corrupt. At least they are learning their numbers this way.

"I'll pick you up at seven-fifteen," David said. He looked almost as pleased as I felt at the temporary reprieve from captivity.

"I don't mind driving. Then you won't have to bring me home."

He looked at me in reprimand. "My Southern-born grandmother taught me better than that. 'David, if you aren't a gentleman, what are you? If you haven't got strong faith and good manners you can't get along in the world,' she says. I've taken it to heart. Why, if she heard, even today, that I let you drive yourself to dinner, she'd be on a plane to the Cities with a wooden spoon in her hand to put me in my place."

"You're doing a wonderful job." I was inordinately pleased to hear that part about having faith. I love good manners in the men I date, but I can live with an occasional affront to Emily Post. Strong faith, however, is something I'm not willing to compromise on. "I'd be happy to write your grandmother a note and tell her what a good job she's done."

His eyes twinkled when he spoke again. "I'll keep that in mind. One never knows when a letter of recommendation might be needed."

David glanced around until he found Chester's whereabouts, on a padded rocking chair across the room, and then, to my surprise, leaned over and kissed me on the nose. "See you at seven-fifteen." He escaped as Chester stood up, the fur on his back upright, hairs marching down his back like soldiers.

I was colliding dreamily with my furniture, trying to make it back to the bedroom where the boys had turned their punishment into yet another game, when the phone rang. I snagged it before going into the bedroom to observe my cleaning crew.

"Suze, it's Darla. What can you tell me about that guy?"

I walked into the bedroom, hunkered down on the floor with my back against the wall, stretched out my legs and gestured to the boys to keep scrubbing. "You know about David." I played dumb.

"Not him, the other one. The weird one."

So she's been thinking of him at work. Interesting.

"Charley? I've been talking about him ever since I got involved with the rescue. What, by the way, was going on between the two of you? I could feel the vibrations eight feet away."

"Nothing went on. He surprised me, that's all. I'm not accustomed to men in pink Mohawks."

"Don't worry—it will be another color tomorrow. How do you feel about burgundy or chartreuse?

"He's kind of cool in a weird sort of way. Not my type, of course."

"Of course." Darla's "type" wears a business suit, tie and alligator loafers. He dines at all the best restaurants, sees all the best shows and drives only the finest cars. Darla may be fluffy looking in her dizzy blond, blue-eyed sort of way, but she's as savvy as a great white shark when it comes to men. Come to think of it, it is *David* who is her type.

"I can't imagine a woman liking that hair of his. The top of his head looks like the back of a dinosaur or the top of a high-security prison wall."

"You are absolutely right," I agreed cheerfully. "Who wants to get up close and personal with a pseudo-reptile? One involved in the theater, no less."

"He's not that bad." Darla backtracked. "I didn't mean…"

"You are just rattled because you were attracted to him and you didn't expect it, that's all. You harbor a prejudice against pink Mohawks and have a preference for Armani suits. Charley caught you off guard."

"Have you ever dated him?" Darla asked, her voice unusually tense.

"Hardly. It would ruin a perfectly good friendship. And," I added slyly, "he's between girlfriends right now."

"Don't be ridiculous. He's not my type."

I don't think David's my type either but I'm still going out for dinner with him.

What *is* my type I wonder? I'm a bungalow-living, animal-loving, sleepwalking clutter-meister whose life is more interesting when she's asleep than when she's awake. How many perfect partners for me can there be in the world?

"Relax and live a little, Darla," I advised.

"Look who's talking. If you relaxed and lived a little you'd be at David Grant's clinic right now consulting with a physician instead of being too afraid to try again."

"You talk like I'm a coward." I felt a flush of indignation fueled by the fact that Darla was right.

At 7:15 I waited outside my house for David to arrive.

"You're lovely tonight, Suze," he said as I slipped into the buttery leather seat of his car. "Almost as cute as you looked in those… What was on those pajamas?"

"Sheep and clouds, thank you very much." I settled in for the ride. "Will I ever get to live that down?"

"Eventually, if you really want to."

"I have so much to live down that I probably won't be alive that long."

He chuckled. "How are the doppelgängers or do you want to talk about it?"

"They are home and I'm not. 'Nuf said?"

"And this night is all for you," David said cryptically.

I was soon to find out what he meant.

As we drove downtown, I silently admired the skyline. I must have been born with either an interior-decorator or peeping Tom gene,

Show other side to operator when boarding the bus.

Keep ticket as proof of payment.

Valid for boarding buses, MAX and Streetcar until time stamped on front.

Must show ID:

- Students grades 9-12 or GED
- Youth ages 15-17
- Honored Citizens

TRI◉MET

Plan your trips at *trimet.org*.
Tickets are non-refundable.

because I always look at the high-rises with their penthouse condos and try to imagine what they might look like inside. I conjure up images of sumptuous luxury, great art and lavish parties, the opposite of what my life is like.

"When you said you lived downtown, you meant it." I watched the impressive skyline of Minneapolis grow nearer.

"I like the city, its energy and culture. I can't say I miss having a lawn to mow and a snow blower in my garage, either."

"Like me, you mean?"

"Don't get me wrong." He smiled at me and the long slashes too-masculine-to-be-dimples creased around his mouth. "I think where you live is great. Cozy."

Good. That told him a lot about me without my ever having to say a word.

His place revealed a lot about David to me as well.

"Where are we eating?" I asked, feeling particularly pampered already as I recalled the menu of tomato soup and grilled-cheese sandwiches I'd fixed for the boys.

"It's a surprise. Someplace you've never been before."

"How can you be sure?"

"Oh, I'm sure. Here we are."

I looked up to gaze at one of the newest luxury high-rises in the city and to my surprise a large door glided open in front of us. David drove down into the bowels of the building that housed the garages. He pulled into a stall, turned off the car and took the key out of the ignition.

"I didn't know there was a restaurant here."

"There isn't."

"Then what are we doing here?"

"Patience, my dear, patience." He got out of the car and came around to my side to hold the door for me.

We traveled to the thirty-fourth floor of the condo high-rise in an elevator so efficient it barely whispered that it was moving. The apartments were built around an octagonal-shaped room decorated with a large wooden table at its center. A massive floral arrangement filled the table. Chairs and small sofas were carefully placed in the area. Most of my house could have fitted into this particular seating area.

David led me to a nearby door and pulled out his key. "This building is only a year or two old but was nearly sold out. I was lucky to get this place." He stepped aside and ushered me inside.

His view was of the skyline of the city to the west and the river to the north. I've seen photographic cityscapes that didn't capture the magnificence the way David's picture window did. Dusk was falling, silhouetting the varied architecture against the western sky. Lights began to sparkle in the buildings and cars moved silently below. The sound here, practically in the clouds, was silence.

Very few of the windows had draperies or curtains. If I love cozy and cluttered, then David adores minimalism and stark simplicity. The room was decorated in masculine black and cream with splashes of red punctuating the room. Paper floor lamps and a black lacquer chest gave the room an Asian feel. A wall fountain trickled a tuneless sound and his one nod to frivolity was an incredible fresh floral arrangement in the center of his glass dining-room table.

His coffee table book was of Ansel Adams's black-and-white photography. Even the candy in the leaf-shaped metal dish appeared to have been left by a decorator who'd been spirited away only moments before we arrived. This place was perfect. Too perfect.

"Do you actually live here?" I blurted before remembering to put on my conversational muzzle. "It looks like a vignette in a showroom."

David, who was standing in front of his stainless-steel, professional-grade, glass-fronted refrigerator looking at the contents, turned his head toward me. "Oh, yes. I think well when things are simple and uncomplicated. Smooth lines lead to smooth thoughts or something like that. Don't you like it?"

"What's not to like?" I countered, not wanting to admit that the stark elegance of the room intimidated me somewhat. I longed for my basket of yarn and knitting needles and an inviting chair with no sharp angles. But the room was beautiful. How could it be otherwise? He'd spared no expense on anything in it. The room was so…so…*David*.

Just as my house was so much an expression of me.

Unfortunately they were two expressions that didn't seem to have a thing in common.

I tried to imagine myself living in this place. The first thing I'd do is hang a few pictures— nature scenes, probably, and those of my family. I also have quite a photo collection of dogs, cats and other critters I've known, loved and fostered. And that velvet Elvis that makes me smile. There was Tommy and Terry's art to consider as well. How could one hang that on a see-through refrigerator door?

And the furniture! Not a rocking chair or recliner in sight. No bunny-soft blankets or squishy, hand-embroidered pillows that say Love Is Just a Dog Away or Shhh! The Cat is Sleeping.

I almost felt pity for David. Leather, chrome, wood, steel, original art hung with surgical precision, the surreal and beautiful view of the city skyline, a television larger than the wall of my bathroom… How could a guy live like that?

By the time I turned around, David had put the entire produce section of his refrigerator on the concrete-topped center island. Three kinds of lettuce, an avocado, grape tomatoes, strawberries, cashews, olives, cheese and a half dozen other things spilled out of a huge wooden salad bowl in a display so colorful it might have been a spread in a gourmet cooking magazine.

"If you want to start the salad, I'll put some dill on the salmon and frost it. It will take hardly any time at all to bake. The rice is already cooking."

"Frost the salmon?"

"With a little mayonnaise. It keeps it moist. Old Swedish trick."

"Are you an old Swede?" I picked up the avocado and a surgically sharp knife.

"No, but one of my grandmothers was. And a very good cook."

"It appears you inherited some of that. This is a very impressive kitchen."

"She taught me everything she knew. Especially how to cook fish. She's also the one who taught me to eat caviar at the age of nine and escargot before the age of eleven."

"Yuk."

"What do you cook?" He looked at me and smiled.

A handsome, intelligent man who can cook—could he get much better than this?

"I make a mean peanut butter and jelly. I grill it. And I have a special ingredient in my macaroni and cheese, pure cream in the sauce. Oh, yes, and I have a meat loaf recipe people would give an eyetooth to get. And cookies— gingerbread, molasses, peanut blossoms and a very fine sugar cookie."

"A real down-home cook, then."

"I'm a real down-home kind of girl." As I said it I recognized how true it was. I also realized that I am the antithesis of David.

Do opposites attract? Maybe. Can they live together? I doubt it. This place doesn't even have dust. Mine, on the other hand has a repository for kitty litter, wood shavings, hay, various

other kinds of bedding and whatever else an unexpected guest of mine might require.

It's a good thing I've already decided I'm
not interested in David Grant. After seeing his
home, I would have had to come to that conclusion anyway. Any man not willing to house a
ferret on a moment's notice is not for me.

David plunged in to help me with the salad
and we were done in no time. The timer rang
just as both the salmon and the rice were
finished. While I'd been staring out the window
earlier, he'd set the table for two with sleek
geometric dishes and a contemporary pair of
candlesticks.

When I dropped my head to pray over the
food, he bowed his head with me. Something,
I guessed, that he'd learned at his grandmother's table.

"You do this so easily and well," I commented. "The salmon is to die for."

"I have to feed myself. I might as well eat
what I like."

"Even the food you enjoy is elegant, like
your home."

He gave me a puzzled look. "What do you
mean?"

"Look at you. You are the *GQ* man personi-
fied, your home is *House Beautiful* and you

move around the kitchen like you learned at the feet of Martha Stewart."

"Thanks, but so what?" He looked genuinely puzzled as to why any of this mattered.

"It says something about you, that's all. Just like the way I live says something about me."

"That you are traditional, creative, inviting, homey and like to build a comfortable nest for yourself?"

"It does?" I did a double take. The way he described it, it sounded downright inviting rather than chaotic.

The discussion turned to other, safe and general, things then—the beauty of the skyline, the plays and movies we'd both seen and restaurants at which we'd both dined.

Chapter Seventeen

After dinner, I sat down on the low leather couch and, to my surprise, found it comfortable. I didn't expect anything made completely of right angles to conform to my body, but the buttery leather hugged me like a fine glove.

"Uhmm. Nice."

"What did you expect?" David took the other end of the coach.

"It looks more uncomfortable than it feels, that's all."

"No squishy pillows and homemade afghans?"

I flushed a little. "I'm a reverse snob, I guess. What draws you to this contemporary look?"

"Spartan look, you mean?" He appeared amused. "Let's just say that I have a lot going on in my head and when I get home, I want my gaze to go around the room and not snag on anything cluttered or fussy, that's all. I tend to look at my work as a constant puzzle to solve."

A flicker of some emotion came and went so quickly I barely picked up on it. "And?"

"And sometimes the puzzle is more complicated than others."

"How so?"

"Although I work primarily as an administrator now, I consult with others in the field. Lately I've had several interesting calls from doctors with clients who have parasomnia disorders, somnambulism, mostly, with occasional night terrors, which can be a troublesome pairing."

"Now say it in English." I pulled a cashmere throw, which was artfully arranged on the back of the couch, onto my lap and cuddled into it. David's eye would just have to snag on the unfolded afghan until he got around to fixing it later.

"Some of the sleepwalking cases I've seen lately have been rather violent."

I swallowed thickly. One thing I'd never been was violent. Except for that time my sister found me stomping on invisible cockroaches on the kitchen floor.

"Surely if you aren't violent when you are awake you won't be aggressive when you are asleep." I almost added, *I hope.*

"That's not the case. What you do when you are asleep taps into another, more primitive part of yourself. What goes on in your mind when you are asleep is not dependent on your waking thought processes."

"I suppose that explains some of my weird activity," I allowed, "but I'd like to think that who I am and the values I have translate into my sleep state, too. I'm counting on not robbing a bank in my sleep because I'd never do it while I was awake."

"Don't count too hard on that. You don't have much control over your mind when you are asleep. When we are awake, we *plan* the things we will do. We make conscious decisions. Sleepwalking episodes are different. They are precipitated or triggered by something rather than planned. It happens when a person's decision-making processes are not present."

"So I could do *anything* in my sleep? Even something horrible?" That thought chilled me more than any danger to myself.

"Plato wrote that 'in all of us, even good men, there is a lawless wild-beast nature which peers out in sleep.' I know of people who have awoken in the midst of attacking their spouse, thinking they were beating off an intruder or being attacked by a wild bear."

"Did the spouses get hurt?"

"A broken nose in one case, a bruised lip in the other. It could have been worse."

I shivered beneath the cashmere wrap. "Let's talk about something else, this gives me the creeps. What else do you do? For fun, I mean?"

He leaned back and put his hands behind his head to think. His shirt pulled against his well-defined torso and my mouth grew dry. I wasn't supposed to be noticing things like this. I'm on a sabbatical from men and David is making it difficult for me to stay the course.

"I'm almost afraid to tell you because you will probably respond like everyone else I know."

"Try me."

"For the fun of it, I'm writing a book on sleep disorders."

"Oh, for goodness sakes...."

"See? I told you that you'd respond like everyone else. What I do during the day for work, I do in the evenings for fun."

"When I think about it, it doesn't seem so strange. You love what you do. Why not?"

"Exactly." He beamed at me as if I were a prize student. "Now what do you do for fun—other than paint man-eating creatures on chair seats?"

"I take in smelly, dirty, frightened and sometimes sick or injured animals and try to heal, clean and love them up. When they're healthy and beautiful, I give them away."

"That's not everyone's idea of fun any more than writing a book might be."

"I also like to run. I've done a few half marathons in the past year or two. Mostly, though, I just do it for the joy of it."

"Me, too. Maybe we'll have to run together sometime."

The idea of seeing David overheated and disheveled in his workout clothes is particularly appealing to me. I don't need to be the messy one all the time.

The question came bubbling out of my too-big mouth before I had time to stop it. "David, do you date?"

"What are we doing right now?" he asked, amusement showing on his features.

I've got to give it to the guy; he certainly takes things in stride.

"I'm not sure. Are you?"

He lounged on the sofa studying me. "I think I'm getting to know someone better in the hope of gaining a new friend. How about you?"

"Ditto," I mumbled, so embarrassed I thought my red cheeks might combust.

"And to answer the rest of your question, I do date. Or have. It hasn't been terribly convenient lately, that's all."

"Dating convenience? That doesn't sound very romantic." Maybe, I thought, I should whip off my sock and stuff it in my mouth so I don't spew out any more prying questions. Still, I've never been known for being anything more than an open book, a what-you-see-is-what-you-get person, and I expect, sometimes futilely, that others will be the same with me.

"I haven't met the right one, I guess." He sounded as if he were turning inward, examining the reasons for this. "That's surprising at thirty-five, but I can be very single-minded when I need to be. I completed college in three years before finishing my M.D. and Ph.D. I've worked in research, had my private patients and taught at the medical school as well. There were a number of years when I had difficulty fitting in time to eat and sleep. Dating wasn't even on my radar."

"And now?" Here I go again, Miss Twenty Questions.

"Now the women I meet have their own lives and agendas. Most are successful in business or the arts. They are single-minded, too."

"But maybe ready not to be *single* any longer, I'd guess." I thought of the women I'd seen hovering near him at the restaurant in Chicago. Most were so glittery and flawless that they didn't seem quite real. Especially not to me who believes if I have time to polish my nails before I leave the house, I started getting ready too early. Of course, David's own home was glittery and flawless. Perhaps he preferred that in his women as well.

"There is that. And there's nothing more terrifying than having a bright, successful, ambitious woman decide that you are her next acquisition."

"I hadn't looked at it quite like that."

"How about you, Suze? What's kept you single?"

For once, I wasn't going to tell the truth. I wouldn't lie, exactly, but this was going to be a sin of omission. I wasn't going to mention that this sleeping issue of mine was a major part of the problem.

"I have had disappointments, that's all. Relationships I'd hoped would turn out haven't." *Men who've ridiculed or derided my sleepwalking sagas and then expected me to trust them. Men who have given me ultimatums such as "It's me or those animals, Suze." And men who want me to be something other than who I am.*

"Just some plain old bad luck, I guess."

He didn't look as if he believed me but instead of pushing me further, he changed the subject.

"There's a run for charity next Saturday. I've got a dozen guys who refuse to run with me but have agreed to sponsor me. If I run the distance, I'll earn almost three thousand dollars for the cause. Do you want to run with me? I'll guilt them into sponsoring you, too." He named the list of charities that would benefit. There were several animal shelters that Charley and I had worked with over the years. They'd all sent their "hopeless" cases to us rather than euthanize the animals without a final chance to find a home.

"I'll do it."

David looked both surprised and pleased. As he shifted on the couch so that he could move closer, I forgot about my sabbatical from men. In fact, I forgot about everything except the fact that he was about to kiss me. And then everything went blank except the feel of his lips on mine.

Whamm! Kapow! Zowie! Zamm! Eee-you! Zap! Wow!

I felt like a character in the Batman comic. He'd swept me off my feet while I was sitting down.

Even he looked surprised when he pulled away. It had been a friendly, tender, affectionate kiss, with surprising results. Neither of us knew what to say.

He recovered first. "Well, that was...I'm at a loss for words. *Nice* hardly says it."

My mouth worked but nothing came out. A completely innocent, friendly kiss that caused fireworks inside my head.

Fireworks in my head and a knot in my stomach. Although I didn't want to, I mistrusted David's motives. I refuse to be a guinea pig and I make a lousy lab rat. When I'd heard the words *I'm writing a book on sleep disorders*, a seed of my doubts and reservations about the good Dr. Grant had been planted.

Maybe sleeplessness is making me loony. Pretty soon I'll be suspecting my new cat of rearranging the furniture when I'm not home.

"Would you like to see my office before we leave?" David asked politely. "I don't let many people see my inner sanctum but you could be one of the privileged few."

"I'd love to." I wanted to see if his work space was as sleek and tidy as the rest of his home.

It was. Only more so. A blotter, a pen and a laptop were the only things on David's vast desk. The entire room held built-in bookcases, the books neatly arranged, protected by glass doors and lit with soft light from inside the cases themselves.

"There are more books here than in a medical library!" It was a medical library of sorts, one specializing in everything written on sleep and wakefulness. "Don't you read anything else? Mysteries? Thrillers? Cookbooks? I've got a half-dozen cookbooks I'd love to loan you."

Nearly three hours had passed when I finally glanced at my watch. "I've got to get back. I promised my parents I'd be home by now."

"Does it matter so much?" He tipped his head appealingly but I shook mine emphatically in the negative.

"Mickey and Jeff have found that their sitters—even my parents—have to be treated like gold. They always arrive home when they promise. It doesn't take much for a sitter they've hired to refuse to come back again so we all step very carefully."

"What about you? They left you alone with them for two months or more. That sounds more like a lump of coal that a brick of gold."

"Their blood runs in my veins and there's no getting out of that. Besides, I love them. I love

all children but these two really crack me up—both literally and figuratively. I'll manage."
Somehow, if it doesn't kill me first.

He helped me put on my jacket and we returned to the garage for our ride home.

We were both quiet, David lost in his thoughts and I in mine. No matter how hard I tried to push it out of my mind, a nagging question remained. Sure, David is wonderful, handsome, considerate and funny; there will be no argument from me on that. But like the poor little rich girl who can't be sure if she's loved for herself or her money, did David really care about me or were my nighttime meanderings too tempting to resist? The last place I want to find myself is in a textbook for physicians or, worse yet, on the shelves of the self-help section at my local bookstore.

I have to be careful. The full reason for my sabbatical from men came back to me. I didn't want to be hurt again.

Chapter Eighteen

"Thanks for the wonderful evening," I told David as we stood on my front porch. "Even though right now I feel as if I've stepped back into high school."

David chuckled and waved at my parents who were peering from behind the curtains on the front window. When he did so, the curtains snapped shut.

"I haven't been monitored this closely since the night of my graduation party." How humiliating. I'm out with a big-shot doctor and my parents are hovering in the background like the parents of a rowdy teenager. My cheeks burned with embarrassment.

"I think I'll go in now, put a sack on my head and cower under my covers for the rest of the night, hoping the humiliation will go away."

"Don't do it on my account. I've had a wonderful evening with you, Suze. Refreshing. Fun." He glanced at the window and put a quick peck of a kiss on my forehead. It burned like a brand into my skull.

"Are you sure you will run with me next Saturday?

"For the sake of the animals, yes."

"Not at all for my sake?" Charm oozed out of him like toothpaste from a tube.

"Maybe just a little."

He chucked me under the chin much like my brother did when he thought his little sister was being cute. Then he ambled back to his car, leaving me more confused than ever.

"How was your date?" Mom looked so eager for details that I felt sorry for her. These people really need more to do.

"Not a date. Just dinner and pleasant conversation. And it was fine."

She looked disappointed. "'Just 'fine'? Nothing more? And he looks like such a nice man, too. And a doctor—a *sleep* doctor, no less!"

Lest she get the idea that *fine* and *mediocre* were synonymous, I told her about David's home, the windows that overlooked the city and his position at the clinic.

Then even my dad got excited.

"He's perfect for you, Suze. He'd know what to do with you when you roamed around at night. Wouldn't that be great?"

Yes, indeed. My parents hope I'll fall in love with someone who can act as my keeper.

"By the way, Mickey called."

"Did the twins get to talk to her?"

"Oh, yes. Terry told her all about eating paste and throwing up at preschool and Tommy told her he'd locked himself in the bathroom for almost an hour and the teacher had to call for help."

"They could have talked all day and not said that. Were the boys upset when they heard their mother's voice? Were they lonesome?"

"Not for a moment. They told their mother they loved it at Auntie Suze's house and that they could stay here 'forever.'"

A cold chill bolted down my spine at that thought.

"That must have made her happy, to know the boys aren't homesick."

"Actually, I think it made it worse. She cried for the rest of the call, wondering what she'd done wrong as a parent since her children didn't want to come back to her.

"We calmed her down eventually but she's lonesome, homesick and impatient."

"Any idea when they'll be back?"

"None whatsoever. That's part of the problem. The waiting is stretching on indefinitely."

"Did you have a good night with the twins?"

"Dandy," Dad blurted. "Couldn't have been better."

"You're going to have to tell her sooner or later," Mother chided. "She'll find out, you know."

Uh, oh.

"You really should clean your garage more often," Dad grumbled. "You can't leave things on the floor like that."

My mind raced through the items that might be in the garage, which is, for the record, practically spotless. The only thing I could think of was some equipment I used to paint the chairs I'd just finished. Paint, of course.

"What happened, Dad?"

"I'm buying you shelving tomorrow. I'll be over to install it next weekend."

"What your father is trying to say is that he turned his back on the boys and they pried open several cans of paint."

"If the concrete in the garage weren't so porous, I might have been able to get more of it up. A skim coat of concrete will make the whole thing look better."

Deny, distract, divert. Why didn't Dad just spit it out, that the twins had trashed my garage floor while under his watch?

"He tried to mop up most of it, but I'm afraid your floor now looks like a modernist painting. Picasso, maybe, or, if I were to go out on a limb, Franz Marc."

I guess Mom does get out occasionally, to the art museum, at least.

Dad brightened. "And none of it got on your car except…"

I closed my eyes. *Tell me it isn't so!*

"And it will wear off the tires in no time flat." He grinned. "'Flat,' get it? Flat tires, flat…"

"I'll put it on Mickey's bill," I sighed.

"You're charging her to watch the twins?" Mom gasped.

"No, but I'm going to show the list to her every time I want her to do a favor for me. That should get me favors from my sister through the year 2050."

"I'm sure you girls will work it out," Mom said reassuringly.

When Dad went into the other room, Mom dropped her composed and unruffled act. "I don't know how you do it, Suze, those boys are into everything. I found them swapping the flour and the sugar in your canisters and then discovered they'd drawn pictures on the inside of every one of your kitchen cupboards."

"My biggest problem is not getting enough sleep," I admitted. "That's when everything starts to get the best of me."

"Are you sure that the doctor can't help you?" She held up a hand to stop me from speaking. "I know, I know, you've spent huge amounts of time and money trying to figure this out already and nothing's worked."

"I'll be fine, Mom. Really."

Then she got a shrewd look in her eye. "Even if you won't agree to follow his direction, you do have your biological clock to think of. He seems like a very nice man, a Christian, too, you said."

I tried hard not to let smoke come out of my ears. "Mom, even if I do have a ticking clock, the twins will no doubt have shut if off by the time I hand them back to Mickey. Have you thought of that?"

After my parents left, I checked on the boys. They were curled, as usual, into a ball so that I could barely tell whose arms and legs were whose. Their cheeks were a perfect pink, their lashes dark against their skin. Each had his own thumb in his mouth tonight. I love them so much when I see them like this, calm and beautiful, I want to weep for joy.

Other times they just make me want to weep.

* * *

In the morning, I ran them to the babysitter early and returned home to get ready for work. I'd been coming in later and later, and working harder and harder while I was there, hoping that no one would notice a decline in my productivity. These morning moments have become the only bit of sanity in my day.

That's why I was disappointed to hear the telephone ring.

I was tempted not to answer it but I didn't recognize the phone number on caller ID and I'm just too curious for my own good.

"Suze? Hi, it's me, David."

My stomach did one of those roller-coaster dips that it does when I'm nervous or excited. I'm not sure which it is David makes me, maybe both.

"Am I calling too early?"

"No, not at all. I'm getting ready for work. The twins are already at day care. I've found it's easier to get ready without them around."

"No doubt." He sounded sympathetic and amused, and that somehow comforted me. He, at least, seems to understand the familial pickle I'm in.

"What can I do for you so early in the

morning?" I asked. He could hardly be calling me to ask me out for breakfast.

"You're probably going to be angry with me, but I have to give it a try. I just came into the office and at our staff meeting, someone mentioned that there had been a cancellation for tomorrow morning with one of the doctors. He's top-notch, the guy I'd go to if I needed a sleep specialist. It will be no problem to fill the appointment because he books out so far in advance that people are always waiting to get in sooner. I wanted to check with you and see if you'd reconsidered seeing someone.

"Not that I'm trying to force or coerce you in any way," he added quickly. "Just giving you the option. After this I won't bring the subject up again unless you ask me to."

"Now that's tempting. Never bring it up again?"

There was silence on his end of the line. He was probably not sure if I was teasing or telling the honest truth. I was doing a little of both, I guess.

"David, you know…"

"I just want you to have the opportunity to see one of the finest specialists in the nation if you wanted to take it. I'm not going to push, Suze. I'm just laying it out for you. In fact, I don't even want you to give me an answer. I'll have the receptionist hold off for one hour before filling the appointment. If you want it, call her within the hour, if not, don't. You'll never hear about it from me again."

I heard some commotion in the room David was in.

"I have to go. Take care." And the line went dead.

That left me staring at the phone wondering what to do next.

Furious, I stomped into the bathroom and turned the shower on full blast and as hot as I could stand it. Then I got in and began to have a conversation, by turns furious, frustrated and frightened, with myself.

"How did he know he could get to me by *not* pushing me? No one else in my family…or even Darla…seems to have discovered that key to my personality."

"He can read you like a book, that's how."

"Why? No one else can?"

"He's smart, that's all."

"If he's so smart, why is he hanging out with you? Why does he care?"

That stopped me mid-scrub.

Why *does* he care? He likes me. I suppose he doesn't want to see me unhappy and he believes he has an answer for me. Maybe... I refused to allow my mind to travel down those lines. I don't know why it's so difficult to be on a sabbatical from relationships. It was easy until David came into the picture. But David and his medical specialty have messed me up royally. If I *do* go to the doctor against my will, I'll resent him. If I don't do all I can to take care of myself, he'll take exception to my behavior. This relationship is doomed already, thanks to my parasomnias.

And why, I wondered, as I scrubbed myself dry with a fluffy white towel—one that hadn't been in the washing machine when the twins dumped a package of powdered Kool-Aid in the tub—was I being so stubborn about this? What could it hurt to just talk to a doctor again? Maybe they had learned something since I'd gone through this before. Could it be I hadn't had the right physician the first time? Perhaps...

I glanced at my bedside clock. Fifty-eight minutes had passed since David's call. Maybe I'd already missed my opportunity.

Chapter Nineteen

My phone was ringing when I walked in the door after work. It was Charley, ostensibly calling to see how Chester was doing.

He didn't fool me for a minute.

"The cat's okay. Getting fatter and his fur is improving. He still has some pretty strange personality quirks and he's psychologically attached to that rag of a blanket he came with. He loves the twins and is growing to love me as well."

"He loves the kids more than you? That's unusual, isn't it?"

"I don't feed him my entire meal under the table, for one thing. He is, by the way, the only cat I've ever met that likes green beans. By the time dinner is over and the boys have funneled everything they don't like to Chester, he waddles out from beneath the table like Garfield after eating a lasagna."

"Why don't you put a stop to it? Should the kids be doing that?"

"I don't cook anything that could harm the cat. And as for the kids, I'm doing my best to spoil and ruin them so that my sister never gets the idea of leaving them with me for three months again."

"Got it."

I waited for Charley to say something else, but he never did.

"Have I answered all your questions or are we going to sit here and listen to each other breathe for the rest of the evening?"

Then the real reason for the call came out.

"Do you see much of that Darla friend of yours?"

"She's been doing a lot of traveling back and forth between Minneapolis and Chicago. She stays with me when she's here. In fact, she's coming in tonight." Which meant I could get a good night's sleep.

Charley sucked in his breath like a human vacuum cleaner.

"Are you all right?"

"Sure. Fine."

"You don't sound fine. You sound as if you are strangling."

"Do you think there's any chance she'd like to see me again?"

"So you've got a crush on her?"

"I didn't say that." He was indignant.

"No? I know you. You don't make a first move unless a woman is more interesting to you than animal rescue or the current theater production.

"I'm sure she'd like to see you again. Do you want to come over?"

"No. I just wanted to know if she'd *like* to see me. I didn't say I wanted to see her."

Shades of junior high.

"Well, she's going to be here a couple days, in case you are interested."

"Yeah, whatever. Thanks." And he hung up.

It must be something in the air. I am getting the weirdest calls from men these days.

Darla arrived at seven, just in time to see the boys polishing off their snacks—ice cream with jalapeño jelly, sunflower seeds and coconut. The seeds and coconut were new to the mix. If I ate that, I'd be up all night but it seems to tranquilize them and make them sleep. I'm not one to argue with success.

Darla, looking every bit the executive tonight, flopped down on a kitchen chair and gratefully accepted a bowl of ice cream sans toppings. "I am so looking forward to a good night's sleep."

"Sorry I didn't get your room cleaned since you were here last." I nodded toward the twins. "It's been a bit hectic."

"That's an understatement, I'm sure."

"Just so you don't mind. I peeked under your bed a few minutes ago. There's nothing but dust under there."

The twins, as if on cue, sat up straight, slid off their chairs and disappeared down the hall, leaving their ice-cream concoctions half-eaten.

"What's going on?" Darla wondered. "I've never seen them leave ice cream behind."

"I don't know, but I'm going to check it out." I stood up to follow the twins with Darla close on my heels.

They'd gone into Darla's room and were both flat on their bellies with their heads stuck under the dust ruffle of the bed. They were giggling and chattering to each other.

Darla and I each grabbed a pair of feet and pulled them out. "What are you guys doing under there?"

"We're looking for butt dust."

Darla and I glanced at each other in confusion. "What?"

"You said there was butt dust under here and we want to see it."

Nothing but dust under Darla's bed. Of course. Butt dust. How could I have missed it?

Darla, meanwhile, doubled over in hysterics.

"Listen, guys, there's a little misunderstanding here. There is no…none of that under the bed. Go finish your ice cream, okay?" They slumped off, the picture of dual disappointment. I could hardly blame them. What four-and-a-half-year-old boy wouldn't want to be the first to discover butt dust?

By the time Darla gathered herself together, tears of laughter had streaked through her mascara. Her blouse had come untucked from her pencil slim-skirt and she looked as disheveled as I did after a day with the boys.

It wasn't until we were sitting in the living room that I brought up Charley's name.

"Do you think you'd like to see my friend Charley again?" I ventured. "You seemed a little interested in him the first time you met."

Darla screwed her face into a frown. "Yeah, I don't know what that was about. When I met him I thought he was cute in a weird, over-the-top way, but I've thought about it since then. I don't think he's my type. It might be interesting to find out though." She picked up the mug of tea from which she'd been sipping. "I haven't had much luck with men I've met lately."

So there's still a chance for Charley. Things were looking up.

"Now if I'd met someone like Dr. Grant that would be different."

"You did meet him."

"But he's attracted to you. You'd have to be blind not to see it. He thinks you're cute and funny." She smiled slyly. "And you are like a science project for him—the woman who walks in her sleep. You're perfect for each other."

My heart sank. I know he thinks I'm "cute" and "funny." That's fine. But that "science experiment" part? It was what I was most afraid of. David is writing a book on people just like me. Is that why he's so interested? Everything in me wants to say no except for a small, intuitive part of me that screams yes.

I was feeling sorry for myself when the doorbell rang. Darla looked up, surprised.

"Are you expecting someone?"

"No." When I turned on the porch light, I saw Charley standing outside, shifting his weight from one foot to the other, looking nervous.

"Hey, buddy, what's up?" I greeted him when I opened the door. I lowered my voice. "Darla's here. Want to come in?"

"I've got a big favor to ask," he blurted.

That usually means he has some unwanted creature he wants me to take in.

"This thing came in tonight and I can't get any of the volunteers to take it so I thought you might…"

"If they won't, why should I?"

"Because you are loving, compassionate and sensitive to the needs of animals?"

"Good try but I'm not buying. What is it?"

"A white rat."

"Charleeeee…" I whined. "You know I don't do *rats*. Besides, you just left me with a cat. You might just be bringing Chester his dinner."

"He's in a cage. All the people who usually take pet rats and mice have their quota. Since you just got rid of Hammie, I thought…"

"I didn't get rid of him. I placed him. How's he doing, by the way?"

"The little girl adores him. He's never been happier. You could do the same for this rat if only…"

"No."

It was if he hadn't heard me. Charley spun and returned to his car. When he came back he was carrying a cage with one very large, very cranky-looking white rat in it.

"I've got a home for it, I think, but they won't

take him until after they get back from vacation. He'll be here two weeks, tops."

"No."

Charley is selectively hard of hearing. *No* is one of the words he chooses not to hear. Instead he loped into my house and put the cage down on my foyer table.

Darla appeared in the doorway. "Hi, Charley. We meet again." She smiled and her dimples winked at him. She looked particularly lovely in her pale pink suit that flattered her peaches-and-cream complexion. I heard Charley suck in his breath.

"Would you like to come in and sit down? I just made tea."

Charley acted as if drinking tea were his number-one priority in life and followed her into the other room like one of the Pied Piper's rats, which, under the circumstances, seemed highly fitting. They sat across from each other and made small talk as if I weren't even in the house. By the time they'd made plans for Darla to sit in on rehearsal for the new play Charley was directing, I knew that something special could come of this. I've known both my friends a long time, and the understated fireworks and nuanced subtext happening between them was something I'd never observed in either of them before.

I did mental cartwheels and clapped my hands as we all walked back to the foyer when Charley was ready to leave.

"So you'll be there on Saturday?" Charley asked hopefully. I haven't really studied him for a while or noticed how good-looking he really is. With no parrot stripes on his head, he looks subdued and handsome. It didn't hurt that he was wearing a Ralph Lauren shirt either. Darla likes that sort of thing.

"I'll have Suze give me directions to the theater," Darla assured him. "I'm really looking forward to it. What's that thing?"

I turned to see what she was staring at. It was the enormous rat Charley had put on my cherrywood table.

"It's just Mr. Snickers. I brought him over so Suze could take care of him for two weeks."

I closed my eyes and waited for the explosion.

Darla's scream burst one of my eardrums and permanently deafened me in the other ear. Charley, who didn't have time to prepare, fell backward against the wall, his eyes wide with horror.

"It's just a rat."

"'Just a rat?' I hate rats! How could you bring him into this house? Get him out, get him out!" Darla glared at Charley. "And you get out, too!

Rats. I never dreamed you'd have anything to do with rats!"

She disappeared into the bedroom while I consoled Charley.

"She's never going to speak to me again, is she?" Charley said weakly.

"It's doubtful."

"Rats, I thought maybe something could come of this." Charley shoved his hands into his coat pockets and left, his shoulders hunched and dejected. Even his Mohawk seemed to droop a little. But he left the cage behind.

Rats is right, I thought as I shut the door.

I leaned against it and closed my eyes.

Well, that went well. Not.

I will never look for a job as a matchmaker, that I know for sure.

Chapter Twenty

"I think I must be crazy. Why am I doing this to myself?"

I stared into my bathroom mirror. I had eyeliner and mascara on one eye but not the other and looked as unbalanced as I felt. It had taken longer than I'd planned to take the boys to the sitter and now I was running at least twenty minutes behind. This was not how I had planned my entrance. Quickly, I finished my other eye, swept on some blush and a little lip gloss, grabbed my purse and hurried out the door.

"It's just a visit. I haven't committed to anything. I'm in charge." I kept muttering assurances to myself all the way to David's clinic. I parked in the lot of an impressive stucco-and-stone building with the clinic logo on the tasteful sign outside.

Why I was doing this I wasn't sure. I didn't want it to be about David. I needed to be doing this for myself.

"I'll give it one last chance," I muttered as I pushed open the front door. "And that's it. If this doesn't work, the next thing I'll do is hire a keeper."

The receptionist greeted me as if I were a long-lost sister and had me fill out several pages of forms before saying, "Dr. Grant is in if you'd like to see him. If not, he told me to tell you he'd be in his office when you got done with your appointment." She looked at me as though I must have miraculous powers to get so much of her boss's time and attention. I was a little curious about it myself.

"Do I have time to say hello?"

"Yes. Dr. Fielding will be with you in about fifteen minutes. Come this way." She led me to the back of the clinic to a suite of offices, knocked on a door, opened it and gestured me in.

"Suze, you came." David stood up behind his massive mahogany desk and walked around it to greet me. He wore a dark suit, white shirt and bold red tie, the epitome of power dressing. The pleasure and relief in his expression was, I must admit, heartwarming.

"Did you think I wouldn't?"

"Frankly, I wasn't sure. I thought perhaps you'd send me an e-mail saying, 'Mind your own business and never speak to me again.'"

"Then why did you do it?" I sat down in the chair he indicated.

He retreated again to the chair behind his desk, sat down and tented his hands together. "Because I felt it was worth a shot. I was willing to risk your friendship for the sake of your getting some help."

Of all the things I expected him to say, it wasn't that.

Before I could speak, a nurse rapped on the door and announced that Dr. Fielding was ready to see me. David slid a piece of paper across the desk to me.

Lunch at the Lagoon after your appointment. Meet me?

I nodded. I wouldn't miss it for the world.

I found him in a booth at the back, private and set apart from the flow of traffic. Just as I arrived, a waitress brought a plate of appetizers and a pot of green tea to the table.

"Perfect timing," David greeted me. "Egg roll?"

I sank onto the bench across from his. "You

must know exactly how long these appointments take to have timed the order so perfectly."

"There are rumors that I run the clinic like clockwork. Maybe it's true."

Most definitely. It ran as smoothly as a door with well-oiled hinges. As determined as I was not to be impressed, I couldn't help it. That faint flicker of hope that I could beat this thing had been fanned again.

"How did you like John Fielding?" David dished up a plate for me and I didn't protest.

"Great. He's smart, funny and seems to know his business." I patted my purse. "And he sent me home with the same old list of instructions. Exercise regularly, avoid caffeine, use a comfortable mattress, blah, blah, blah."

"You're a pro at this, I know, but give him a chance. He knows his stuff. Forty million people have chronic sleep disorders, another twenty million have occasional problems and there are more than eighty different disorders. He's seen plenty of them in his office."

"You must be very busy at your clinic then."

He laughed. "Busy enough. But enough shop talk. How are the boys?"

"Wait a minute." I stopped eating mid–egg roll. "Aren't you going to ask me any questions?"

"No. I'm not your doctor. Medical things stay between you and Dr. Fielding unless you want to discuss them."

The man could be a psychologist. He knew perfectly well that I was bursting with questions and *now* he didn't want to talk about it! Instead he was calmly ordering pork fried rice to go with our meal.

"You're the man who is writing a book. Don't you have anything to say?"

"Did you know that dolphins would drown if they fell asleep? They need to be awake to control their breathing."

"Then why are there any dolphins left?"

"They have the ability to sleep one hemisphere of the brain at a time."

"So they can somehow be awake and asleep at the same time?" I pondered the thought for a minute. "That's a little like me, isn't it?"

"You are very unique, Suze. Not many people are so active in their sleep as you are. You are a very interesting study."

I picked at my rice and sweet-and-sour shrimp but didn't say more. Suddenly I didn't feel like eating. *An interesting study.* Yep. That's me. The nagging hunch that David found my disorder more intriguing than me was back. And that book he's writing—did I fit into it somehow? I instantly regretted agreeing to see Dr. Fielding.

"David, you're a Christian…."

He nodded, looking curious.

"What do you think about Proverbs 11:1?"

He looked at me inquisitively. "'The Lord hates cheating, but He delights in honesty.' Is that the one you mean?"

I was more surprised that he knew it than I should have been. I really didn't trust him, did I?

"Yes, it is."

"I've based my life and all my business dealings on that verse. It's one of my favorites. I like clear direction and no-nonsense requests." There were furrows in his brow, put there by me and my question. "Why?"

"Just wondering."

"That's a pretty odd thing to be 'just wondering.'"

"I think a lot about honesty and integrity these days. I have to decide if I should tell my company how severe my sleepwalking is. Maybe they'll decide they don't want me in the new position." I skewered him with a look, determined to test his response. "I don't like fabrications of any sort—or undisclosed agendas—if you know what I mean."

Like making me Exhibit A, for example.

But of course he didn't know. He had no idea that I was leery of showing up in his book as one of his worst-case examples. Even if no one ever read the book or recognized me in it, I would feel violated. But he did know Proverbs 11:1. That counts for something. Maybe my worries are all in my head.

Feeling miserable, I finished my lunch and went back to work. I want to trust David, but I don't, at least not yet.

Darla certainly doesn't trust me anymore, or Charley, either. She thinks we're both demented to even care if the rat lives or dies. She steers clear of the laundry room. And she insists on keeping the door closed to that room as well. This is a good thing, especially for the rat.

Chester, now acclimated to my home, is getting a fat belly that swings near the floor when he walks. His fur is shaping up and all the nicks and cuts on his body have faded. One wouldn't even guess now what condition he'd been in when he came to me. And now he has a purpose in life, something for which to live.

Unfortunately, his purpose is to eat the rat in my laundry room. When I came home from work today I found the door open and Chester splayed across the rat's cage as if he'd been pasted there. His voice was scratchy from growling and even his tail looked tired from flicking.

I pried him off the cage one toenail at a time and carried him in the other room to feed him something less tasty than fresh rat. Then I returned to the laundry room to study the rat.

He'd realized that no matter how fierce Chester sounded, he could not get to him. Mr. Snickers was leisurely nibbling on food in his dish and daintily lapping up water with his pink tongue. His blasé attitude must have driven Chester crazy.

I retuned to the kitchen and called Charley.

"You have to come and get this rat—or the cat—they can't cohabitate any longer. No, it can't wait a few days. Now. I'll be expecting you within the hour." And I hung up.

That meant, of course, that Charley would be here at dinnertime and would expect a meal in payment for driving to my place during rush hour. Resignedly I began to put together my semi-famous spaghetti sauce.

He and Darla arrived at the same time, just as I was putting spaghetti into a pot of boiling water. She stared daggers at him and he looked loopy and lovesick right back at her.

"Dinner's ready. Darla, set the table. Charley, fill up the water glasses. I'll pull the garlic bread out of the oven." Keeping them busy seemed the only way to keep them apart.

The first half of dinner was icy. Then an earth-shaking yowl broke into the silence.

"The cat got into the laundry room again. You've got to get his prey out of here."

We dashed into the room to see the cage toppled over. Chester was lying underneath it looking surprised and unhappy to have a rat sitting on top of him. "See what I mean?"

Without another word, Charley picked up the cage, opened the back door and trotted to his car with the rat in hand.

"Thank goodness that creature is out of this house," Darla murmured, sagging against the wall. "What kind of a man can tolerate a rat?"

"Charley respects every living thing. Sometimes it gets to be a problem but mostly I respect him for it. He's a truly gentle man, Darla. You'd know that if you'd give him a chance."

She shuddered. "I don't want to hold hands with someone who has touched a rat."

"Better than holding hands with some guy who *is* a rat," I muttered.

She should know; she's dated plenty of them.

She looked at me strangely but didn't speak. Something had made her wheels start turning.

Charley returned looking sheepish and went to wash his hands in the bathroom while I removed the spaghetti plates and dished up spumoni.

Darla cleared her throat. "I'm sorry I seemed so angry the other evening when you brought that rat to Suze. I'm terrified of rodents. I moved out of a house once because I heard mice scratching inside the walls."

"No problem," Charley responded magnanimously. "They aren't my favorite, either, but when someone brings a pet in—any pet—I treat them the same. Suze is the only one I can count on not to be squeamish."

I took my time, putting the cookies on a plate and making tea for Darla. Things were looking up in the dining room.

Chapter Twenty-One

Saturday and the 10K arrived too soon.

Darla, who runs at an indoor track in Chicago, decided that she, too, would enter the race since David's friends had agreed to sponsor not only David and me but also any of our friends.

Once Charley got wind of that, he suddenly morphed into a track-and-field man himself, insisting that he was in tip-top shape and would have no trouble making the run either. The last time *I* can remember Charley doing anything that faintly resembled exercise was last January when the Siberian husky he was fostering decided he wanted to be on the opposite side of Lake Harriet from Charley. The dog, born and bred to pull, had, due to Charley's refusal to let go of the leash, towed him into the middle of the lake. Charley running on ice, skidding and sliding to keep up, was an Olympic moment. Or one for *America's Funniest Home Videos*.

Darla stomped into my room looking mad and beautiful in her running shorts. "I'm being stalked." She went to the mirror and began to draw her lips in ruby-colored lip liner.

"Anyone I know?" I opened a drawer to find that the twins had dismantled all my paired socks and re-paired them, one light and one dark to a set. Thankfully Mom and Dad had taken the boys for the day.

"You introduced me to him."

"Charley's not stalking you. We've hardly seen him lately." I eyed her suspiciously. "Are you sure what you don't mean is that you *wish* he'd start pursuing you?"

"The man dresses like a parrot! Not my idea of Mr. Right."

"He's almost done with that gig."

"What is he going to be next, animal, vegetable or mineral?"

"Just plain old Charley is a pretty nice guy."

Darla made an odd snorting noise through her nose to signal her disbelief.

"I think you're acting like you don't care about him because you know that you could really fall for the guy."

She looked at me with horror written on her face. "You don't believe that!"

"It doesn't matter what I think. Do you believe it?"

She opened my drawer and took out a ponytail holder to tame her curls. "The man I marry isn't going to need remedial lessons in wardrobe selection."

"Don't judge a book by its cover."

"Or a man by his suit coat?"

Darla sat down on my bed and sighed. "He's cute, but he's *so* not my type."

"I hear you there." I dropped down beside her.

"David Grant, huh?" She pulled back her hair and put it into a springy ponytail. The curls began to escape from their confines almost immediately. "He's not such a reach for you, Suze. But Charley and me? No way."

"There are…issues…with David."

"What do you mean?"

"I'm not sure I trust him."

She stared at me as if my head had tipped off and I was holding it in the crook of my elbow. "The man is Mr. Ethics. He's well known and respected, famous, even, in the world of neurologists. What's not to trust?"

"He's writing a book."

"That's more awesome still."

"It is also why I don't trust him." I sat down on the bed and began to put Vaseline on my heels and the bottom of my feet, anywhere I might develop blisters. Then I pulled on my running socks, which are padded on the bottom. "I do not want to show up in his book."

"He wouldn't do that. Anyway, what's the big deal?" She grabbed my Vaseline and began to work on her own feet. "You do sleepwalk and everybody knows it. It's hardly a secret."

It was hard to argue with that.

"I know that this won't make sense to you, but I'm still touchy about it." I spelunked around in my mind for the words that might help her to understand. It wouldn't be easy, I knew, looking at the disbelieving expression on her face.

"Ever since I was a kid, people have enjoyed sleepwalking stories at my expense. It gets old after a while to hear about myself doing ridiculous things and it's not easy to respond with 'I was ridiculous, har, har, har,' all the time. I didn't *want* to be weird."

"But ever since I've known you, you've always laughed about it." She stared suspiciously at me. "Or was it laughing on the outside, crying on the inside?"

I averted my eyes.

Darla grabbed me by the shoulders and hugged me. "Oh, Suze, I didn't know! I never realized…." She made me look at her and there were tears in her eyes. "But I should have known, shouldn't I?"

Now I felt even more vulnerable than ever.

"You couldn't have. My goal was to make everyone think that I didn't consider it all that big a deal. I know that even my family doesn't know the true extent of how I felt. I don't think I've ever thought of myself as 'normal' or 'whole.'"

"You may have felt that way but you are about as normal as baseball and apple pie."

"No, I'm as normal as a circus sideshow and you can't convince me otherwise. How many others do you know with six or eight large locks on their doors to keep themselves in, not others out?"

"Everybody has something that makes them feel different or set apart. Have you thought that you might be taking it more seriously than you should?" She quickly added, "Not that it's not serious, of course, but maybe, a little shift in perspective would help?"

She hadn't seen me on my knees, hugging my makeup kit, toothpaste oozing all over my pajamas, in front of David. No, I have a clear-eyed perspective on what this somnambulism thing is all about. It's everyone else who has it mixed up.

I laced up my shoes and stood up. "We aren't going to settle this today so we'd better get going."

"Just for the record, I think you're wrong about not being able to trust David. You won't show up in his book without your permission. You know that."

"Later, okay?"

"It's your life, Suze. I'm here for you no matter what." Darla gave me a quick hug. "I'll grab my bag and meet you in the car."

After she'd gone, I stared at myself in the mirror. Clear skin, rosy lips, eyes that seem to smile even when I'm not; nothing had changed since the last time I looked at myself.

"She's right," I told my reflection. "And you know it."

No time to think more about it now. The object of my turmoil was at this moment waiting at bib pickup and wondering if I'd ducked out of the race.

David in sweats and with tousled hair is a beautiful sight to behold. Being a casual girl myself, I liked seeing him ruffled and natural. If anything it made him even more attractive to me and, frankly, I'm not quite sure how I feel about that.

"Uncertainty is your middle name," I muttered to myself. "Get a grip."

I took a deep breath and a step toward the object of my confusion.

His gaze took me in as it leisurely skimmed my face, my cherry-red tank top, black spandex running shorts and the white running shoes that made my feet look as large as icebergs. He took a step toward me and I felt my heart speed up. Terrific. Just being around him was cardio. What would running with David at my side do for my heart rate? Good thing he's a doctor. I might go into cardiac arrest.

"You are beautiful today." He kissed me on the lips then held out his hand. "Let's pick up your bib and entry packet before it gets too busy."

I did as he said and Darla joined us as we walked to the start area. Runners were intently stretching, their expressions serious. Everyone was getting their game face on for the challenge. A tent selling everything from Gatorade to running shoes had music blaring from a loudspeaker. A carnival atmosphere prevailed.

As we walked, I noticed all the attention David received from the female runners.

Some stood a little straighter, others smoothed back stray hair and smiled. David was oblivious to it all.

Soon, however, all attention moved away from David and onto another man racing down the hill toward us, shoelaces flying, baggy nylon shorts flapping around his knees.

Charley, couldn't you have found some decent clothes for today?

He was the exclamation point on Darla's statement that he was not her type. She was standing a few feet away from me, checking to see if her shoes were tied perfectly while good old Charley came at us as though he were being thrust out of a wind tunnel.

Of course, even if he'd been modeling the *GQ* of running attire, he still had the Mohawk. He'd stopped painting his head a couple days ago and his scalp was now covered with a fine peach fuzz of dark hair, but he still had a shortened version of the haircut riding proudly atop his head.

Darla saw him and her eyes widened and, I'm almost positive, she cringed.

She moved closer so that no one around could hear.

"What on earth is he looking like that for?"

"He's okay. There are other people wearing shorts like his." Well, one, maybe, and he was pretty out of shape and may have been coerced into joining this charity run.

"Looks aren't everything, Darla. And, despite his weird get-up, he's cute."

"You don't want me foisting David onto you and yet you are doing the same thing with Charley and me."

"There's potential for you and Charley, that's all. I know his heart and I know yours. They are more closely matched than you think and a lot more in step than just your appearances."

"Come and tell me about it when you decide to give David a chance." Darla flipped her blond head as if to say "Take that."

What an odd little game we had started here, trying to foist off unlikely men onto each other because we each thought we knew something the other didn't.

Charley loped up to us like a happy puppy, his shoelaces still dangling. "Sorry I'm late. I got a call to pick up some abandoned Lab crosses. By the time I got them to the shelter, I didn't have time to go home and pick up my running clothes." He looked down at his billowing shorts. "Do these look too stupid?"

Darla opened her mouth to speak but I silenced her with a glare.

"You could be wearing aluminum foil and

duct tape and I'd say you looked great if you just rescued a litter."

He smiled so sweetly that I hoped Darla had seen that irresistible expression.

"Thanks, I knew you guys would understand."

I glanced at Darla and was glad to see she looked discomfited. Good. Maybe she'd realized she'd jumped to judgment too soon with Charley.

Still, as we were readying for the sounding shot that would start the race, Darla made sure both David and I stood between her and Charley.

With only seconds before the start, David leaned toward me and kissed me on the cheek. "For good luck," he said softly.

As it turned out, I didn't need all that much luck. It was Charley who did.

He hung back a second when we started moving, coming around us from the back and insinuating himself next to Darla, where he jogged happily alongside her. It took her a few minutes to realize who it was close on her heels and when she did, she gave a figurative revving of her internal engine and sped up, leaving Charley, literally, in her dust.

He might have been a match for her if he'd been running daily as she had but as it was, all he got for his efforts was a stitch in his side, a red face and the opportunity to eat a lot more people's dust as well.

We didn't see Charley again until we'd collected chunks of bread, bananas, oranges and bottled water from tables in the finishers' area and settled on the grass to rehash the race.

He was barefoot and limping as he moved toward us. I saw a huge water blister on one side of his foot but he was smiling widely as if he'd come in first instead of nearly dead last. He flung himself onto the ground next to us and said, "What a great race!"

Darla, who was in the act of pretending she'd never seen him before, stared at him. "Why? You must have come in 249th in a field of 250!"

"Yeah, I know. But the greatest thing happened. I walked beside an older gentleman who was just doing this for the fun of it, like me. I told him about the shelter and he asked about my hair so I also told him about my parrot gig. He thought it was the funniest thing he's ever heard. Turns out, he's a former schoolteacher himself who has come into some money." Charley lowered his voice. "Significant money. And he's coming over next week to see our facility. If he likes it, he may consider giving us a sizable donation."

Charley flattened out on the grass. "I had no idea that a 10K would be such a great place to network."

Darla was looking at him again, I noticed, but with new respect in her eyes.

Chapter Twenty-Two

"Charley is full of surprises, isn't he?" Darla and I shared the mirror in the ladies' room of a coffee shop while the guys purchased lattes.

"You just noticed?"

"He's just so different that it's hard to get past his look."

"And now you have? What changed?"

"That man he met, the teacher he introduced us to before we left the race area? The way he and Charley talked, so passionately and professionally, about the importance of humane treatment of animals and about teaching it in schools like Charley's been doing? It made me look at him in a different light, that's all."

"Does that mean you might be interested in him after all?"

She turned around to face me, ignoring the

other women moving in and out of the room. "Suze, am I judgmental?"

"Is this the time or place for this conversation?" I asked. "Can't it wait?"

She ignored me. "I've been avoiding a really nice man just because I made up my mind about him without even knowing him." She checked her makeup again and sighed. "But I still think that someone with my tastes and experiences might not mesh very well with his likes and dislikes. Don't get any ideas that I'm serious about him. He is making me think, however."

"Isn't compromise what it's all about? Two people who come into a relationship with a 'My way or the highway' attitude won't make it, but if they can meet in the middle they have a chance."

"Meet in the middle?" Darla looked doubtful, trying to imagine what a middle ground with Charley might be.

"He grows normal hair and promises to dress nicely in public, you quit being so uptight about his crazy impulses. He promises to quit bringing rodents and reptiles into your house or the shelter and finds a foster home that will take them directly and you quit nagging him about three hundred pounds of dog food in the garage, stuff like that."

"What about you and David?"

"What about us? That's different."

"How?"

"More complicated, that's all."

Darla pressed her lips together but the look on her face told me that this was a conversation I'd be having again later.

David and Charley were waiting on the patio, visiting comfortably, as if they'd known each other for years. David could converse with anyone and Charley has never met a stranger, so it seemed perfectly natural that they would bond even though they were a neurologist and a man who enjoyed imitating a parrot.

When Charley saw Darla, he jumped up so quickly, he knocked over his chair and created a loud clatter. Darla, who hates a scene, closed her eyes and took a deep breath.

I could see Darla trying to get her mind around the idea of give-and-take with Charley. If he wanted her in his life, he was definitely going to have to give up being a klutz in public.

"Auntie Suze! Come see what we did!"

That's another request that sends cold chills down my spine, especially from the Terror Twins. Fortunately, this time it was not a disaster in the making.

Darla, who has natural and creative mothering skills, was helping them to set up a lemonade stand in the front yard.

"What are you doing, taking a swipe at commerce or the entire U.S. economy with this?"

"They want candy. I told them if they wanted it, they'd have to buy it themselves."

"Good plan." The twins and processed sugar are a highly combustible mix. I try to keep them far apart.

"So then they wanted to know how to make money and, voilà—" she swept her hands open "—a lemonade stand."

"Who's buying the lemonade?"

"You, of course, I'm teaching them about earning money, not about net, gross and bottom-line expenses. That will be your job."

I sank into one of the two lawn chairs set up behind the card table/lemonade stand. "Do you think my sister is ever coming home with that baby or has she found it so quiet and relaxing in South America that she's decided to stay permanently?"

"It does seem like it is taking a long time."

"Eons." I took her hand. "And I don't know what I would have done without you these past weeks."

"It's not been that difficult. The boys don't wake up at night and I've only caught you sleepwalking a time or two."

"But you probably saved me from burning down the house," I said grimly. I'd done a bit of sleep cooking last week. I was rolling out sugar cookies when Darla discovered me. Fortunately I hadn't turned on the oven.

"Don't worry about it. I enjoy staying here. Besides, it's given me plenty of time to look for housing. I've liked not having to rush into anything."

"And you don't live far from Charley while you're here."

"What's that supposed to mean?"

"I think I've seen you doing a little 'compromising' the past week or two. Dinners out. A movie now and then."

"We don't go to either fast-food drive-throughs or five-star restaurants, if that's what you mean. And he's willing to give up movies about ax murders if I'll give up those with subtitles."

"How is it?"

Darla smiled and her face softened. Sunlight danced off her golden hair and she was radiant. "Good, Suze. It's good."

"And how is it for Charley?"

The sunlight in her expression dimmed a

bit. "I'm not sure. He seems happy. His hair has grown back and he's even more handsome than I thought he'd be, but he doesn't say much about us. It's as though he's skating on thin ice and holding his breath, hoping he won't break through."

"Can you blame him? You're an intimidating package, Darla—bright, beautiful, successful…."

"Insecure, afraid to hope…"

Almost simultaneously, we put our elbows on the table and our chins in our hands and sighed. "I thought we'd get over this after high school," I muttered.

"I thought I'd gotten over it permanently," Darla responded. "What's happened?"

"I think the old anxiety and lack of confidence is back because we care. It's easy to be self-assured in relationships when you aren't really in love. You don't feel vested in it and if it ends, it ends. But if you really love someone and are terrified it might not work out…"

"So you're saying you're in love with David?"

I eyed her. "Are you saying you're in love with Charley?"

We both sighed and put our foreheads in our hands, and as one voice we pronounced, "Oh, rats!"

Chapter Twenty-Three

I'm going to quit going to David's house. It's too depressing for me. All that sterile, open space, all that cat fur–free furniture, all that perfectness. Besides, it makes me feel like a hypocrite. I gave Darla the big lecture about compromise and accepting people as they are and she's actually *doing* it. And me? Hypocrisy is my middle name.

Why worry about a speck in your friend's eye when you have a log in your own? How can you think of saying, "Friend, let me help you get rid of that speck in your eye," when you can't see past the log in your own eye? Hypocrite! First get rid of the log from your own eye; then perhaps you will see well enough to deal with the speck in your friend's eye.

Ouch.

I can advise Darla for hours on how she and Charley can make their relationship work, about giving up something in order to gain something, about how true love acts.

Then, when I turn the floodlight onto myself, I flinch. What will I give up for David? I love my cozy, sentimental, comfy home just as much as his angular, sleek, sophisticated six-figure condo in the sky pleases him. I can't give up the animals. They're my passion. Chester is actually turning into a cat. Instead of looking like a moth-eaten pelt, he's fat and sleek and has a cocky tip to his head. He's still got some species confusion and thinks he's a watchdog, but because I miss Chipper, I've let him delude himself into thinking he's actually protecting me and my house.

And what would David do if I brought home to his elegant condo a half-dead ferret or a dog with mange? Could I even get it past the doorman who looks as though he was imported for duty from the marines? He looks at me suspiciously now and all I've tried to sneak into David's place is a batch of white-chocolate macadamia-nut cookies.

Or the mustache cups, backside-eating chairs and my grandmother's rocker? And I haven't even mentioned the twins, who could make

David's place into one large coloring book in a matter of minutes.

Oil and water don't mix. If David is oil and I'm water, we've got trouble.

As Darla grows more and more happy in her unlikely pairing with Charley, I grow inversely more miserable. Perhaps it's for the best that David is often out of town presenting educational and training programs across the country. I need time to think.

The phone rang about 9:00 p.m. The boys were asleep and Darla wouldn't be home for at least an hour. Although I was tempted to ignore it and go to bed, I picked it up instead.

"Suze? Hi, it's Mickey."

"Hi, sis. How are you?"

"So homesick that I can hardly stand it. How are the boys?"

"Asleep."

"Those little darlings."

Darlings. Right. The boys don't so much fall asleep as drop in their tracks. It takes energy to create chaos and mayhem twelve hours a day.

"What's the latest on the baby?"

"She's so beautiful, Suze. We spend time with her every day. As soon as the paperwork is complete, we'll be home. Have you been talking about the new baby with the boys?"

"As best I can. So far they would prefer a puppy or, if that doesn't work out, goldfish."

"You've got to prepare them, Suze! If their mommy and daddy are gone for weeks and then come home with another child, what will they think?"

Although I didn't say it, I know the answer. They will assume Mommy and Daddy did them a huge favor by letting them stay with their weak-willed aunt and they will decide that they want to live here instead of at home. After all, there's no cat at home, no lemonade stand and no doting aunt. Not only that, they love Darla, who is their all-time favorite playmate. I'm afraid that Mickey might be in for a rude awakening.

It appears that David may see me in my sheep-and-cloud pajamas again whether I like it or not. Dr. Fielding wants to do a sleep study, which, from experience, is an oxymoron. If I can't sleep well at home in a cozy bed with dark shades, a night mask and soothing rainforest sounds, how will I sleep in an unfamiliar twin bed in a cramped room with electrodes clamped all over my head? If patients don't have sleep disorders when they arrive, the tests will give them some. What's more, I don't like people watching me while I sleep and I know perfectly well what that one-way mirror in the room is for. Tonight I'll be the prize monkey in the zoo. Let's hope they don't invite too many bystanders to view the entertainment.

"Now just ignore these wires if you can," a cheerful but deluded technician told me as he hooked me up to machines. Cameras would film me in the night. Suddenly the nights on the floor by my bedroom door before Darla came to help me with the twins seemed like the good old days.

She pointed to a single rose that sat on the bedside stand in a slender crystal vase. "What's this?" Briskly she moved toward it as if to pluck it up and banish it from the medically sterile room. Then she glanced at the card propped against it and her hands fell away as if she'd been burned. "Oh." She eyed me with new interest and respect. "Isn't that sweet?"

After she'd gone, I picked up the card.

Suze, have a good night's sleep. See you in the morning. David.

Beneath it he had added a quote from *Macbeth. Lo you, here she comes! This is her very guise; and, upon my life, fast asleep. Observe her; stand close.*

Oh, great. Somewhere something was

probably recording the way my heartbeat sped up at the sight of Dr. Grant's handwriting.

I lie there willing my mind to stop whirling. Finally I began to tick off the things I'd accomplished in the past sixteen hours. Breakfast with twins. Vacuumed oatmeal off floor and scrubbed walls. Bathed twins. Mopped up bathroom floor and put fans in hallway to dry the carpet outside the bathroom door. Took twins to day care. Assured woman that I would pick them up early so she could lie down for an hour before supper. Also assured her that their mother would be coming home soon. Although her fingernails were digging into my flesh as I left, I did not make up a false date just to soothe her jangling nerves. Finished several open projects at work. Employment is a piece of cake next to caring for twins. Picked up twins. Delivered them to their grandparents' house for safekeeping. Met Darla at gym to run. Picked up twins from my parents' house. Assured my parents that my sister would be home soon and they would no longer have to watch twins on the evenings I run.

Running…

I was running but couldn't seem to get anywhere. Gradually I realized that I'd made my way to the top of the world and was looking down from high over the Arctic. I could see the outline of the continents below, spinning on their earthly orb. Terror struck me as I realized that it was not the earth below me but a gigantic globe with all the earth's land masses hammered in copper. The space where the seas and core of the earth should reside was void. I balanced on the brink over the vast emptiness below. My foot slipped and I fell, tumbling over and over into the cosmic emptiness below me, shrieking, clawing and waiting to be swallowed by the abyss.

I woke up screaming and pulling electrodes off my skull as a nurse and a technician burst into the room to calm me.

Well, that was pleasant.

"I think we've got enough," the technician said. "No more electrodes tonight. Just try to rest normally. When you awake in the morning, you can just get dressed."

Try to rest normally? I thought as I dozed again. What did she mean "rest normally?" What had just happened *was* normal for me.

In the morning I awoke gradually, wondering for a moment where exactly it was that I was. Slowly the night came back to me. I rolled off the bed, went to the sink to splash water on my face and then pulled on my clothing. Surprised that no one had come to check on me, I opened the door of the sleep lab and peeked into the hall.

I had no idea what time it was. Obviously it was before the clinic officially opened for the day, since no staff was about. I did hear two low male voices laughing and talking somewhere down the hall so I went in search of the technician I'd seen last night, hoping she might be with him.

As the voices grew clearer, I paused. A familiar voice was speaking.

"So then there's this amazing crash when the shelves fall over and land right on the car. They'd been pushed of course, and the damage was enormous. Insurance didn't want to cover it and…"

I paused, my heart in my throat.

"It's a great story for the book. I've got to use it."

"What else have you got? Is there anything I can do to help?" another voice inquired. "I'm really looking forward to seeing your book come out. I think it will make the public aware of just how common these issues are. It's been needed for a long time…."

Slowly, silently, I backed away. Shelves?

Landing on my father's car after I had tried to scale them? I'd dreamed I was rescuing a kitten sitting on the top shelf. That was *my* story! One of the few I'd shared with David. And he'd told it to someone else who thought it would be a great story for the book.

I felt cold, betrayed and furious. Deceived and wounded. How *dare* he? *How dare he?*

"How was your night at the sleep center?" Darla greeted me when I opened the door and bolted into the house.

Though my fury had not subsided, I was determined not to show it. I pasted a faux-cheerful smile on my face. "Same old, same old."

"When do you talk to the doctor again to see what he has to say?"

"They said they'd call me."

If, that is, I go back at all. I would have to be very sure that David Grant was nowhere within a three-hundred-mile radius of that clinic before I'd even consider darkening their doorstep again.

"You look funny. Upset. Are you okay?" Darla peered at me, her brow beetled.

Darla's glowing these days. According to her, she and Charley are "communicating" and "compromising" all over the place. Charley's auditioning for less edgy, trendy roles and may have a shot at a local production written and produced by a theater that our Restwell Insurers contributes to financially as a gesture of community goodwill. Darla has agreed not to work on Saturdays and they've negotiated a "date night" during which she will turn off her cell phone and not check either her e-mail or her lipstick.

It's nauseatingly sweet compared to the mess I'm in.

I *told* David I didn't want to turn up in his book in any way, shape or form yet, unbelievably, I heard him laughing and discussing my story while I was supposed to be sleeping just doors away.

Now what am I to do? Acting as if nothing has happened is impossible. Telling anyone what happened is unacceptable. Seeing David again is intolerable. The only thing left is to become so frenetically busy that no one can observe the turmoil I'm experiencing.

It wouldn't be difficult, I decided. I had the twins to help me out.

We spent mornings at the park, swinging, jumping, picking up leaves and sticks, lying on the grass and listening for the buzz of insects. We spent afternoons at the zoo, the science museum, the children's theater and at kiddy matinees. And we spent evenings at my parents' house or at the rescue center so that I was not home to pick up David's calls. Each night I would delete his messages unanswered. Darla, gaga over Charley, spent most of her free time with him at the center or rehearsals and seemed not to notice much of what I was doing.

One evening, nearly ten days after I'd overheard David's betrayal, as I listened to the messages on my answering machine, I accidentally let one of his messages play too long before deleting it.

"Suze, I have to know what's going on with you." His voice was clipped and angry. "I know you're avoiding me and I have no idea why. I've tried to do what I thought you wanted. I haven't pressed you about the results of your tests. I've been your friend and this is what I get in return? No explanation? Nothing?"

I winced at the fury and the hurt I heard in his voice. David wasn't a man accustomed to being crossed. I'd really set a bridge on fire this time.

"I'm going out of town for a few days and when I get back we're going to settle this. I'm terribly disappointed. I thought maybe…you

and I…we might… But I guess I got that
wrong. I don't like to leave things open-ended.
If you have something to say to me, I want you
to say it. Then I'll leave you alone. Permanently." And the phone slammed back onto the
receiver.

I should be happy, I thought, as I sank onto
my couch. He is as done with me as I am with
him. Instead I felt wretched. I lay down on the
couch and wept.

Eventually small fingers pried open my eyelid
and Tommy peered in. "Auntie Suze crying?"

I reached out and snared the little boy with
my arm and tickled him. "Auntie Suze is okay.
Just feeling sorry for herself, that's all."

I sat up and Tommy wormed his way onto
the couch beside me. "Why?"

"Somebody lied to me and hurt my feelings."

Tommy's mouth pursed into a round red
"oh."

"I don't lie," he assured me.

"That's good. Where's your brother?"

A worried expression creased his smooth
features as he processed his next statement. "I
don't lie."

"Then tell me where Terry is."

And with the saintliness of George Washing-
ton announcing to his father that he could not

tell a lie, even about that hacked off cherry tree in the backyard, he said, "Helping you."

I sat up a little straighter. "Helping me what?"

Tommy edged away a bit, just in case I didn't take the news as well as he hoped I might. "Paint the garage."

Chapter Twenty-Four

I couldn't get the idea of the sleepwalking Lady Macbeth out of my head, so I turned to the works of the bard to read exactly what Shakespeare had said.

Doctor: I have two nights watched with you, but can perceive no truth in your report. When was it she last walked?

Gentlewoman: Since his majesty went into the field, I have seen her rise from her bed, throw her night-gown upon her, unlock her closet, take forth paper, fold it, write upon't, read it, afterwards seal it, and again return to bed; yet all this while in a most fast asleep.

Doctor: A great perturbation in nature, to receive at once the benefit of sleep, and do the effects of watching! In this slumbery agitation, besides her walking and other actual performances, what, at any time, have you heard her say?

It wasn't exactly comforting.

Neither is thinking about David.

The door slammed and I heard Darla come into the house. I could hear a second pair of footsteps behind her. Charley's.

By the time I got to the living room, Chester had attached his teeth to the leg of Charley's pants. He's become very halfhearted about being a watchdog and now sleeps through most visitors. As his health returns and he feels more secure, he has a real desire to become a lap cat, something fat and cozy that doesn't even open its eyes when a stranger comes in. I give him another month, at which time he will become a portly, lazy lout like the rest of his kind. I can hardly wait.

"What are you guys doing here?"

Darla tossed her purse on a chair. "We're here for an intervention."

"What's that supposed to mean?"

"Why have you been avoiding David?"

"Who says I have?"

"Give me a break," Darla said. "I'm busy, not

blind. Besides, I've picked up a few of the calls you've ignored. He's a great guy. What's wrong with you?"

"So it's *me* that something is wrong with? Have you ever thought for a moment that it might be something with him?"

"No," Darla said bluntly. "I haven't. He's not the one with the hang-up about your sleep issues. You are."

"What's that supposed to mean?"

"You're so self-conscious about what happens at night when you're asleep that you don't enjoy your days, that's what. So what if you sleepwalk? So what if you do crazy things that make others laugh? Is that so bad? You've never said a mean word about another human being. You are the kindest, most gentle, compassionate person I've ever met. You'd do anything for me or any of your friends. Your amazing faith is a model for the rest of us. You're creative, inventive, imaginative, artistic, compassionate and beautiful.

"The only problem you have is that you're a legend in your own mind."

What? "I don't get it."

"Of course you don't." Now it was Charley's turn.

"You've always let it bother you that you do

crazy things in you sleep. You act like it makes you less than everyone else. Well, here's the big news, Suze, you're the only one who thinks it's a problem."

"A legend in my own mind? Pretty harsh, don't you think?"

"You're walking away from a great guy, Suze. If it's because of this sleep business, you're going to regret it for the rest of your life."

"You don't know anything about it, either of you. David *betrayed* me."

"Him? No way," Charley protested. "The Boy Scouts aren't as reliable as he is."

I gave him a dirty look.

"What's this awful thing he's supposed to have done?" His voice was heavy with doubt. For the first time ever I felt as if he wasn't on my side.

So I told him the same thing I'd told Darla, how David had said in no uncertain terms that he was going to use *my* story in his book after he'd promised to be my friend.

Charley heard me out but didn't looked convinced.

"And?" Darla said.

"'And' what? Isn't that enough? He betrayed me!"

"How do you even know it was you he was talking about? Did he say your name?"

"He didn't have to, Charley. I know what happened to me."

"Have you talked to him about it?"

"Of course not!"

"Why not?"

"I'm too angry to face him."

"That's not quite fair to him, is it?" Darla picked up my Bible from the coffee table and flipped through it until she found whatever it was she wanted. She put her finger on a spot and began to read.

"'Dear friends, if a Christian is overcome by some sin, you who are Godly should gently and humbly help that person back onto the right path. And be careful not to fall into the same temptation yourself. Share each other's troubles and problems, and in this way obey the law of Christ. If you think you are too important to help someone in need, you are only fooling yourself.'

"The least you can do is ask him why he did it, Suze."

"Frankly, I don't think he 'did' anything." Charley sounded so certain as he said it that I had to take notice. "Suze, you're accusing him of something he wouldn't do, professionally, *couldn't* do. I've never known you to be unfair."

Interventions are very uncomfortable things.

Darla and Charley's meddling forced me to sit back and reevaluate my entire life.

A legend in my own mind. That's pretty egotistical sounding and it has troubled me all day.

I picked up the telephone to call my parents. I had something important to ask them.

Dad answered.

"Hi, Pops. What are you doing today?"

"Cleaning the garage. Your mother thinks it's untidy."

"Is it?"

"Of course not, it's a garage. They're supposed to look like this but it's easier than convincing your mother otherwise."

"Dad, do you remember the time I pulled some shelves over on your car while I was sleepwalking?"

He hesitated. "Vaguely. You were trying to rescue something you thought was on top of it, if I remember correctly. A rabbit, maybe?"

"No. It was a kitten."

"Hmmm." He didn't seem very interested.

"Did it upset you a lot that your car was damaged or that insurance didn't want to pay for it?"

"What are you talking about?" He sounded genuinely bewildered. "The car was barely scratched and the guy at the body shop is a friend of mine. I didn't turn in an insurance claim. It didn't cost me a dime."

"Then how…" I recalled the words I'd heard at the clinic…. *The damage was enormous. Insurance didn't want to cover it….*

"Then why did I think that I'd dented it so badly?"

"You were always like that as a little girl. I've never known a child who tried to be as 'good' as you did. Any time anything went wrong you blamed yourself. It was a particular problem because every time you did something unusual in your sleep, you were twice as upset about it as anyone else and would blow things out of proportion. Of course, you did have some doozies…."

I let my father regale me with a few incidents before I asked to speak to my mother.

She came on the phone quickly and sounded out of breath. "I've got your father cleaning the garage and I don't dare leave him alone out here," she told me cheerfully. "So I'm weeding flower beds. That way I can check on him occasionally and make sure he's on task."

I don't question how their marriage works. Whatever they're doing, it seems to be right although far be it from me to want to babysit *my* husband while he cleans the garage. If I ever get a husband, that is. The opportunity is dimming rapidly.

"Do you recall when I messed up your flowers in my sleep?"

"Of course, but Mickey did a much better job of it when she was awake. She and her little friends picked every one of my blooming flowers for a 'wedding' they were going to put on in the backyard. My gardens looked dreadful that year. I'm surprised you don't recall. We talked about it all summer long."

Oh, I recall it, all right. I thought it was *me* who'd spoiled my mother's beautiful flowers.

"Did I do a lot of damage in my sleep?" I asked, my heart thumping wildly in my chest.

"Some, but you were such an angel when you were awake that it made up for all that and more. We were just frightened you'd hurt yourself, that's all." Mom paused to consider. "I wonder if we didn't make too big a deal of it at the time. Then, over the years, it became such a topic of conversation that I suppose some of the stories were embellished. I'm sure if you'd complained or seemed to mind, that would have quit, but you never said anything."

So, by my silence, I had given express permission to let the stories continue?

"Your brother was the worst, you know. That

child spent more time in the corner for telling tall tales. Sometimes we wondered if you actually did some of the things he told you you'd done. Oh! Your dad is calling. I have to go, sweetie, I'll call you later."

I was left with a dead phone line and a readjustment of everything I'd believed about my childhood.

Chapter Twenty-Five

"Darla, how bad was it to live with me in college?"

She stared at me uncomprehendingly. "Not bad at all."

"What about the sleepwalking?"

"It could get interesting, if that's what you mean. Sometimes, though, you talk as if you did it every night. You didn't, of course. It always got worse around exams and when you were under stress. Thinking back on it, if I'd known then what I know now, I believe I could have predicted when it would happen. Midterms, finals, after you broke up with a boyfriend." She snapped her fingers. "Oh, and whenever you signed up for a half marathon or even something as small as a 5K. You were terrible then. We could hardly keep you in bed."

She eyed me suspiciously. "Why do you ask?"

"I have an appointment with Dr. Fielding tomorrow. I just wanted to tell him everything I can think of about my behavior."

I'd made sure that David was out of town before I'd set the appointment. Fortunately the receptionist is quite a chatterbox and didn't seem to question why I was asking when he'd be in again. Maybe I feel guilty about ignoring his calls. My resolve is crumbling. I'm beginning to think that I may have made a big mistake not giving David a chance to explain himself.

Not only that, I miss him.

The twins, miraculously, are shaping up. They don't cause nearly the trouble they did when they first arrived. Having two quasi-mothers around—Darla and me—instead of just one, has taught them that they can't get away with everything they want to do. They are good little boys and don't intend to be mean, so by channeling their energy in new directions, they are becoming practically, and I use the term loosely, well-behaved.

Right now we're practicing for the day their parents arrive with the new baby. It's not going well yet but I still have hope. I thought back to this morning's rehearsal. Tommy was on the couch holding the life-size baby doll meant to represent his new sister.

"Tommy, you can't hold the baby upside down."

"Why?"

"Because babies don't like it and it's not good for them."

He'd studied the doll in puzzlement. "I like being upside down."

"It's fun." Terry toppled off the couch doing a monkey imitation, scratching himself in the armpit.

"Take my word for it on this. Turn the baby around."

In doing so, he dropped the doll on its head on the edge of my coffee table, knocked my cup to the floor and no doubt gave the baby a serious concussion.

Maybe Mickey and Jeff shouldn't come home yet. We have a long way to go in the big-brother department.

Everything about another visit to the clinic reminded me of David as I sat in the waiting room to be called into the doctor's office. With each moment that passed, I grew more miserable. It was David who'd been concerned enough to get me here and I'd mistrusted even that.

I needed my head examined, all right, but when I was awake, not asleep.

"You can come back to Dr. Fielding's office now."

I followed the woman who'd called me through the building. We walked by David's office on the way. His door was not closed and taped to the front of his desk was a picture Terry and Tommy had colored for him. They'd told him it was a picture of me—in my blue-haired, bandy-legged, punk-rocker days, apparently.

What startled me even more than his having saved the picture was the fact that he'd taped it to his desk, his immaculate cherrywood desk. *Sweet.*

I'd told Darla not to judge a book by its cover but I obviously hadn't taken my own advice. Maybe David's perfectionism hid more from me than it revealed.

Then I was swept up in greeting by Dr. Fielding.

"What did you discover?" I got straight to the point. "Tell me the bad news first."

The doctor looked at me oddly. "There is no bad news."

I almost laughed before I realized he was serious.

"I've been looking over your chart again and I have a couple questions I'd like to ask." He frowned a bit as he studied the report. "I see you have occasional migraine headaches."

"Not often." *More when the boys are with me.*

"Dr. Grant told me that you'd run a 10K with him. Do you do much running?"

Odd questions, I thought. What did these have to do with sleepwalking? "Not as much as I'd like. I try to fit it into my day the best I can."

"Do you run in the morning?"

"No, I never have. I'm a night owl and I prefer to sleep as late as I can. Normally I do it after work or whenever I can get to the gym. My friend and I have been running in the evening lately."

"I see."

What, exactly, was it that he saw? It was clear as mud to me.

"There's no doubt you're very active in your sleep," he went on in sublime understatement, "so it's important to look at what might be triggering the episodes. We'll have to do some detective work. If we can connect your sleep-walking with something that is happening to you during the day, it will help us determine what your triggers are. Were you particularly stressed? Was it something you ate, etcetera? Were you under undue pressure? There may be several things going on with you that are creating a confusing picture but I'm confident that we can straighten it out. Now here's what I would suggest...."

I thought back to what Darla had said about my being worse before exams or when I was having trouble with a boyfriend. Hmmm...

"You mean that's all there is to it?" I asked when he was done. "Some blood tests, treating the migraines and not running in the evening?"

"It's slightly more complicated than that, but the medications on the market since you last went through an evaluation should make it easy to control." He smiled at me sympathetically. "And all that time you suffered with embarrassment and fear of doing something to harm yourself or someone else." The compassion in his eyes was palpable.

"I, for one, am able to say that I know exactly how you feel. You see, I'm a sleepwalker, too."

"You are?" I was dumbfounded.

"Yes. Some of those stories you told about yourself? I could say the same things only it may have been worse for me because my fraternity brothers egged me on. If I hadn't fallen off the side of a building, I might actually have crawled into a second-floor office and stolen test scores from a chemistry class." He smiled and his eyes twinkled. "That would have made it much harder for me to get into medical school."

"So you *do* know what I mean."

I was still absorbing the full impact of that when he added, "I've been giving Dr. Grant lots of material for his book. He's a stickler for privacy and not revealing anything that might identify a patient but I told him I'd *like* to be a part of the book. I want the word out there that people like us can be helped."

"You didn't happen to have an experience with some shelving and a car, did you?" I ventured nervously.

"Six thousand in damages on a car that I toppled some shelves onto." He winced. "One of my more expensive mishaps. I suppose I should be glad there weren't more."

"Have you told Dr. Grant about this?"

"Of course. We discussed it not long ago, about the time you came in for testing."

You're a legend in your own mind, Suze.

I was easy to room with unless I was under stress, according to Darla.

And my mother? *You were such an angel when you were awake that it made up for all that.*

And what had put me under stress? Worrying about sleepwalking, no doubt. Maybe I was the cause of some of my own problems after all.

My head was still spinning when I met Darla for lunch.

"What'd he say?" she asked eagerly. "Can he help you?"

"He thinks he can."

"Fabulous."

I retrieved the notes I'd taken in the clinic and laid them on the table. "He made it sound easy. Both migraines and the fact that I work out at night make it worse. It may be hormonal. He says there are several new medications on the market since I was evaluated before and he wants me to try relaxation tapes before I go to bed. And I have to quit worrying about it."

"That's it? No brain reconstruction or beds made like straitjackets?"

"Very funny." I sat back and stared at the single crisp sheet of paper in front of me. "He said I was 'straightforward' and 'easy to help.'"

Darla whistled. "If you're easy, then who is difficult to help?"

I can't name names, but at least I didn't, like the good doctor, try to rob an ATM in my pajamas or set my own house on fire.

Ironically, now it is my turn to wish David would call me. I owe him an apology but so far he hasn't responded to the messages I finally left for him.

In months and years past, the stress of it would have probably made me a moving target around my own house but now, I rarely move at night. The medication, according to Dr. Fielding, is working perfectly.

Too bad it can't undo my behavior toward David.

Chapter Twenty-Six

Home alone, I relished the unfamiliar moments of tranquility. Sometimes it's difficult to remember silence when one hasn't heard it for over two months. In fact, it can be a little unnerving sometimes, especially when one is not comfortable with her thoughts, as I am today.

When Darla and my mother took the boys for haircuts, I jumped at the opportunity to stay home. Last time we went in for a trim, the owner of my salon suggested that I never bring the twins in again, at least not together. Perhaps they can find a more kid-friendly, damage-proof shop. I gave them my full blessing to try.

So, instead of trying to cajole a hyperactive child to sit still for five minutes, I was sitting in a lawn chair with my eyes closed, enjoying the warm, late spring day dreaming of David and how I should have done things differently. Sometimes dreams I have when I'm awake are even more painful than those I have when sleeping.

"What happened to the boys? Did your sister come home?"

I twisted off the lawn chair at the sound of the male voice. David towered above me, blocking the sun. Had I dreamed him into reality? I could make him out only in silhouette, his wide shoulders tapering to a narrow waist, his already long legs even more elongated by my skewed perspective. He looked gigantic, forbidding—and wonderful.

I scrambled to my feet, my heart thudding in my chest. I knew how I wanted our meeting to be. My hair would be glossy, my makeup flawless and my clothes... Well, so much for that fantasy. I was wearing a ponytail, lip gloss and a pair of khaki shorts teamed with a camouflage-print T-shirt and looked more like G.I. Jane than a Hollywood starlet.

"David, I didn't expect you..."

"I decided I'd better come to you because you don't seem to pick up my calls."

"But I left several..."

"I don't know what is going on with you, Suze." He sounded frustrated and angry. "We need to settle this between us so we can both move on." His jaw was set and a frown marred his features.

Move on? So he had decided to rebuff my apologies on his answering machine and come here to end it once and for all. It serves me right, I suppose, but that reality did nothing to stem the tide of emotion that flooded every cell in me.

"David, there are so many things I want to tell you. I made a mis—" But before I could even blurt out the word *mistake* a cacophony erupted inside my house. Charley, who had entered through the front door, pushed open my patio door and walked outside. "There you are."

He was carrying a large laundry basket lined with a blanket. The basket was shifting from side to side in his arms, yipping and squealing. Chester sat at the screen door and yowled while the neighbors' dogs on both sides of my house began to bark.

Charley walked over to us and put his load on the grass in front of us. The basket was filled with fat, squirming puppies. The rescued Lab crosses, by the look of them, yellow, chocolate and black, with round bellies, soft ears and black noses like little gumdrops.

"Hi, David, long time no see."

David, bemused, thrust out his hand to shake Charley's. "What's this?"

"Some careless owner didn't spay his dog and she had a litter of ten pups." Charley's usually benign expression was hard. "If I were making the laws, he'd be paying a fine for this."

"If you were making the laws, he'd be in jail," I corrected. Charley's passion for animals knows no bounds and his sympathy for bad pet owners is nonexistent.

"I thought maybe you'd want to take a few until we can find homes. They're really too young to be weaned and they can't be placed yet—even if I could find homes for ten puppies in a rush."

"Charley, have you forgotten? I've got the twins. Don't you want me to get any sleep at all?"

"I'm desperate, Suze. Can't you…"

"I'll take a couple," David volunteered.

This silenced even Charley.

"You? But don't you live in some fancy building downtown? How could you take puppies?"

"They're small and I have an enclosed balcony they can run in. They're too young to train so all I'd need is a mountain of newsprint for the time being."

I looked at him in admiration. This man had owned puppies in the past. He knew the ropes.

"They'll mess things up," Charley warned. "Puppies can be a dirty business."

"I also have a cleaning lady." David bent down, picked up one of the pups and snuggled it on his shoulder. The pup promptly put its tongue in David's ear. "Besides, things have been a little…quiet… at my house."

"Don't you go out for dinner or something?" Charley asked, still in shock. "Why would you need puppies?"

"Feeling like a homebody, I guess." David gave me a sharp look. "Not that anyone really cares."

"Wow, you aren't the kind of guy I thought you'd be," Charley marveled.

"And what kind of guy is that?"

I felt like crawling in a hole. Any ideas Charley had about him, David would know had come from me.

"Suze told me about your great place. It just didn't sound like somewhere, you know, homey, a place to have pets."

"Maybe I've changed. Perhaps 'homey' is my new style."

Charley accepted that as if it weren't a complete turnaround in David's image. "Okay, sure." He looked at me. "Suze, have you still got that plastic kid's swimming pool? I'll put the puppies in something larger." Without waiting for an answer, he sprinted toward my garage.

"You don't have to take them, you know." I put a couple of the pups on the grass to roll around. They were so fat they looked like gold and brown sausages with tails.

"I want to." He studied me but there was no warmth in his eyes. "I don't think you know me very well, Suze. But you certainly like to decide what it is I think."

"No, David, this isn't about you. It's *myself* that has been a stranger to me." I locked my gaze with his. "It's me I need to get to know. I hope I've discovered that in time."

My words piqued his interest. At least he didn't walk away and leave me with all the squealing pups.

Darla was the next to add to the confusion. She and my mother returned with the newly sheared boys. The twins immediately tumbled to the ground, rolling with the armload of puppies Charley had loosed. Mother eyed David slyly before turning her attention to rescuing the pups from the twins.

My father, here to pick up my mother, meandered into the yard next. He seemed unfazed by the commotion, taking it as an everyday event.

"What is this, a family reunion?" Charley inquired. "If each of you will take two puppies to foster, I'll have my problem solved in no time."

David negotiated himself closer to me as the yard grew more crowded. "I'd hoped to talk to you alone," David said quietly. Counting the puppies, there were already eighteen of us present.

"Get in line," I sighed.

Before David could respond, my father clapped him on the shoulder. "So you're the fellow we're hoping my daughter brings into the family."

David's eyebrow tilted upward and he glanced at me. I shrugged helplessly. My life is totally out of control. Let him try to figure it out. Maybe I could get him to forgive me if I pleaded insanity. Looking around my yard, anyone could see how I'd been driven to it.

"Tell me, David," my father said chattily, "since you understand sleepwalkers, did Suze ever tell you about the time she ran into the neighbor's house wearing only her underpants and a smile?"

"Dad, you're saying that like it happened yesterday. I was only four years old!"

David didn't seem to hear me. He grinned widely, enjoying being sucked into the madness.

Chester, still hearing the sound of canines in the backyard, skulked at the patio door, trying to get a glimpse of the foul beasts, the dreaded demon dogs. When Mother opened the screen door to go into the house, he bolted out, past her, around David and my father and straight up the oak tree in my backyard.

When Chester got as high as he possibly could, he looked down, realized he was scared of heights and began to meow piteously.

"Well, there are three big strong men out there, get him down!" my mother yelled from the kitchen. "I'm going to make lunch."

Mother's in the kitchen; Chester's in a tree; Charley's up a ladder; David's in shock and the twins are… Oh, no. Where are the twins?

We found them in the tool shed my father had left open when he'd gotten the ladder to rescue Chester. I don't have much in the way of gardening equipment or carpenter's tools, but they had found a large glass jar full of nails and a magnet that was entertaining them royally. Tommy, in his pale yellow shorts, had sat in a spot of spilled WD-40, which had permanently blackened his backside. Terry had tried to help his brother clean up and had the rest of the oil smeared across his hands, arms, white shirt and the lower half of his face.

Not so much damage, really, when I consider what they could have done if they'd found the hammer and saw.

David watched me distract and direct the boys back toward the puppies before coming up behind me to touch my arm.

Darla, now on the ladder and holding a can of cat food, was still trying to coax Chester down from the tree.

"How do you do it?" David asked with wonderment in his voice.

"Do what? This is a relatively normal Saturday afternoon for me."

"That's exactly what I mean. Can we talk? Privately?"

I pointed to the gazebo in the back corner of the yard.

I was grateful for the cover of vines that hugged the latticed walls of the octagonal outdoor room. Privacy, at last.

David dropped onto the bench that circled the inside of the gazebo and I sat across from him. What I wanted to do was touch him, so the distance was not only useful but necessary

"I came here, frankly, to attempt to put an end to whatever has been going on between us," he began, "but now I've lost my will. You and your life are fascinating to me, Suze. Even though you don't seem to care to be around me, I want to be around you." He appeared puzzled by the admission. "And I'm not quite sure why."

"Chaos theory?" I offered unhelpfully.

He leaned back on the bench and studied me. "What are we going to do about us, Suze?"

I held up my hand to stop him from going further. "Before you say another word, you have to hear me out. I need to apologize. I know you aren't interested in the ones I left on your answering machine, but I want to try one more time…."

"What apologies? I haven't had a message from you…." Comprehension began to dawn on his face and a flush started up his neck. "Ever since the power outage in my building. I had a note on my door concerning it when I got back from my speaking tour."

So he hadn't received my brief embarrassed calls.

He raked his long, well-formed fingers through his hair. "I just assumed that no one had called. It never occurred to me that the system might have been wiped clean." He looked genuinely grieved by the idea. "I figured that your silence was your way of saying get out and stay out of my life."

"We're real athletes, you and I, always jumping to conclusions." I moved across the gazebo and took my place beside him. "Maybe I'd better explain what precipitated this."

Now it was my turn to blush. "I woke up early the morning after the tests in your clinic and started down the hall to find the technician. That's when I overheard you talking to someone about real-life examples for your book."

"So? They had nothing to do with you. Dr. Fielding has been a great help to me in that area."

"But I didn't know that." I bowed my head and stared at the planked floor. My voice was only slightly above a whisper when I spoke again. "You see, when I was a child, I, too, knocked over a set of shelves in my father's garage. I dreamed I was rescuing a kitten and they toppled onto my father's car."

"I recall you mentioning it. A remarkable coincidence," David murmured, "but not impossible. Many of my patients report similar night activities. Usually it involves rearranging furniture or removing clothing from a closet and strewing them around the house, but I've heard of rescuing small animals before. The brain is a mysterious entity. The more we know about it, the more we realize we don't know."

"When I overheard the conversation, I thought you were talking about me."

He looked horrified. "You thought it was you we were discussing?"

I hung my head.

"And that I'd betrayed your privacy?"

"I'm sorry, David. I should have known better. You've never given me any reason to believe that you're anything other than a consummate professional. I realize now that I've been so hung up on this issue that it's skewed my thinking on several things. I'm so sorry I doubted you."

I didn't want tears to come to my eyes but I couldn't stop them. I'd messed things up royally now.

Worst of all, I realized, my lack of trust in David—or anyone—has spilled over into my relationship with God. What's happened to me? When had I quit clinging to the verses that had guided so much of my life? *Cast all your anxiety on Him because He cares for you.... Trust in the*

*Lord with all your heart, and do not rely on
your own insight. In all your ways acknowledge
Him, and He will make straight your paths.*

It all seemed so clear now, the way that, these
past weeks, I had edged God out of my life.
When had I last prayed about what was happening
to me? Other than church and Sunday school
for the boys, I'd put my relationship with Him
on a back burner and hadn't even noticed.
Shame leaked through me. I'd let my disorder
rule and overwhelm me. "Oh, *me* of little faith!"
I paraphrased aloud. And look where it had
gotten me.

A showdown I'd had with Terry yesterday
popped into my mind. He, not wanting to listen
to my instruction to turn off the television, had
spun to face me as he stood in front of the tube.
With cartoons playing behind him, he struck a
pose, hands on hips, stubborn resistance on his
babyish features. "You aren't the boss of me!"
he informed me. "My *mom's* the boss of me."

Well, *God's* the boss of me and I've been just
as stubborn and resistant as my little nephew.

I looked up, hoping for some type of absolution
and forgiveness but none was forthcoming.

That was, in part, because another disturbance
seemed to be brewing in my backyard.

I glanced out of the doorway of the gazebo in time to see Darla clutching Chester to her bosom and struggling to back down the ladder to terra firma. My father, who was helping her, nearly knocked her off the ladder when my mother let out a piercing screech that left small children deaf in three counties.

My first thought, my only thought, when someone screams these days, is that the twins are either in trouble or causing it. David, apparently on the same wavelength, jumped to his feet. He grabbed my hand and we raced to the source of the ruckus.

My mother had her back to the twins, who were sitting angelically in the molded plastic pool of puppies. It wasn't them, then. They were actually as well behaved as I'd ever seen them.

She was staring at the patio door.

"I have got to lock my front door," I muttered to David. "Too many weird people are getting in that way."

"These 'weird' people are your family," he reminded me.

"But weird, nevertheless." I looked at him hopefully. "You can see now why I'm such a basket case. It's environmental. All my role models are wacky, too."

"I'm beginning to believe you're right." He frowned and stared past my mother to the house. "Who's that?"

The impetus for mother's screams stepped out of the house and onto the porch.

Mickey, holding a plump pink bundle in her arms, and Jeff, stepped into view.

Hallelujah! Praise be to God! They were home safely with my new little niece.

The second thing for which I was immediately grateful was the fact that the boys were no longer my responsibility. I'd kept them alive all this time! And me, I was alive, too. Oh, yes, suddenly there was much to be thankful for.

Chapter Twenty-Seven

David and I had entered the gazebo as antagonists and emerged as allies. Now it was us against them. "Them," being Darla, Charley and my family, who collectively lost their minds at the sight of the new baby. The twins, on the other hand, were not terribly interested in either the baby or their parents. They were, of course, being licked by ten small pink tongues and inhaling the heady and distinctive scent of puppy breath.

My mother hugged Mickey and simultaneously maneuvered the baby out of her arms, leaving Mickey free to rush to the boys.

"Mommy's home, Terry! Mommy's home, Tommy! Come to Mommy."

The boys shifted their attention to the madwoman racing at them. Terry began to squeal with glee and Tommy joined in.

I hung back with David at my side until the shrieks and tears subsided and Mickey's gaze fell on me.

She charged toward me with such fervor that I was tempted to step behind David to protect myself. When she reached me, she squeezed my cheeks between the palms of her hands. "You are the most wonderful sister in the entire world. The boys look amazing. They've grown two inches since I've been gone. And I love their new haircuts but it makes them look so grown up. Were they good? Did you have any trouble?"

There are some questions that are best left unanswered.

Then she grabbed David's hand. "You must be Dr. Grant. I've heard so much about you. You're even more handsome than my sister... Ouch... What did you do that for, Suze?"

I removed the toe of my shoe from her instep, hoping my hint would shut her up but it was not to be.

"You must be very special. Before I left, Suze told me she was giving up men."

He looked at me. "No kidding?"

"You can talk to me later, sis. I want to hear everything but right now, I just want to hold my new niece."

* * *

It was past the boys' bedtime before Mickey and Jeff made their move to leave. The twins had spent most of their time trying to wear the soft black and fuzzy hair off little Maria's head with kisses. The baby, apparently gifted with both patience and a cheerful disposition, took it all in stride.

"Isn't she beautiful?" My brother-in-law leaned over her as she lay in her bassinet.

"Incredible. And perfect. Look at those fingers, and that nose…."

Jeff unexpectedly gathered me into his arms. "We'll never be able to repay you for what you've done for us, Suze. It was you who made it possible for us to take the time we needed to get Maria. When you have kids, you're never going to have to hire a babysitter. We're here for you, kiddo."

I noticed David watching this touching scene with a mysterious smile on his face. Maybe he was thinking what I was. I have a lifetime supply of babysitting to count on and no present or future opportunities to marry. Perhaps I could suggest Mickey and Jeff get me a day at the spa as a thank-you gift instead.

After everyone had gone—the boys to sleep in their own beds for the first time in weeks, my parents to recharge so that they could spend tomorrow with Maria, and Darla and Charley to the coffee shop down the street—David and I took seats in my suddenly silent living room.

I didn't know quite what to say and he seemed content with the silence so we simply sat, watching each other, waiting for what would come next.

David spoke first. "Perhaps I was a little too quick to judge. You did have good reason not to trust me."

"But you didn't deserve it. You've never been anything but kind and forthright with me. It wasn't fair and I was wrong." I paused. "David, will you forgive me? I know I don't deserve it, but I would feel so much better...."

"'Remember,'" he quoted with a smile, "'the Lord forgave you, so you must forgive others.' And there isn't anything to forgive. It was a misunderstanding, that's all.

"Suze," he continued. "How do you feel about the life I live?"

It was hardly a question I'd expected but it didn't take me long to formulate an answer. "It's too perfect."

"What do you mean?"

I made a sweeping motion with my hand to indicate my living room. The twins' toys were everywhere. I'd put my wildly painted chairs near my fireplace and Chester had pulled several scraps of quilt fabric out of a basket and into the center of the room. "What do you think of *my* life?"

"Eclectic. Out of the ordinary. Creative."

"Somewhere you could live?"

He shifted in his chair. "Not easily," he confessed.

"Well, there you have it," I concluded glumly. "David and Suze, the human equivalents of oil and water."

"Emulsions," he said softly.

I stared at him. "I don't understand."

"It's the mixture of two unblendable substances, like there are in mayonnaise or margarine."

"So it can be done?"

"In a sense, with effort."

"You're getting a little too technical for me. I work for an insurance company, remember? You're the doctor."

"It's like you and me, Suze. There's no way we're going to blend our lives without effort."

Who said anything about "blending" lives? I could barely believe that David was still talking to me.

He saw my confusion and smiled. "Darla gave me your lecture."

"Which one? I have so many," I joked weakly.

"The one about compromise. The one that made Darla and Charley decide they could make it as a couple."

"She told you that?" I was surprised. "I wonder why."

"Because she said that if she and Charley could do it, anyone could, even us."

"Us? A couple? Even after the bumbling I've done?"

"Especially because of the bumbling you've done." A playful expression flickered on his features. "Imagine how much helpful information I might gather for my other patients and their spouses now that I've fallen for someone who exhibits their problem."

Had I heard him correctly? Fallen for someone? That someone being me?

"It's one thing to be an expert in sleep disorders and quite another to fall in love with a woman who manifests them," I reminded him, wanting him to be very clear about what he was proposing.

"If we compromise, I think we can make it,

Suze. What do you think? Do you want to give it a try?"

Oh, boy, do I!

Epilogue

Marriage? It's all about compromise.

Our wedding was amazing. The Terrors were ring bearers and they didn't set anything on fire, topple any flowers or even really misbehave. For the briefest moment, I almost missed their old behavior, but I came to my senses within minutes.

Baby Maria stole the show but I didn't mind. I was too busy crying with happiness and giving thanks to God for all the amazing things He'd brought about.

Darla and Charley were our attendants and spent most of the day taking notes for their own wedding. They were trying to compromise about where to hold it. Charley wanted to get married at the zoo and Darla in a large downtown church. I think they'll settle on the cozy church I go to.

David and I both sold our homes and purchased a warm, inviting but contemporary home on a small lake. It's the best of both worlds. The public rooms in our house—the living and dining rooms and foyer—hold David's beautiful angular leather furniture. The kitchen, the craft room and spare bedroom were mine to decorate. The two painted chairs look fabulous in the guest room.

He drives a BMW and I a van that David calls my purse on four wheels. It's filled to the brim with things I might need—sun block, a shovel, books on tape, mittens, newspapers, even a snack or two. And David thinks his BMW is cluttered if his sunglasses are lying on the seat.

I've agreed not to foster any pets that are not of the cat and dog variety. This did prevent me from fostering one adorable pot-bellied pig, but Charley wanted him at his house anyway. In exchange, David lets me have as many cats and dogs as I can manage.

That's one fewer now that I've adopted Chester and given him his forever home.

Of course, I've got *my* forever home now, too. It's in David's heart.

* * * * *

Dear Reader,

Sleeping Beauty was inspired, in part, by the fact that I was an occasional sleep-walker as a child. I didn't get into nearly the trouble Suze Charles finds, but I did wake up once sitting on a footstool in the middle of my family's living room with all the lights on and no idea why or how I got there. The experience never left me. I like to be in control of my world, and the idea that I could do things and go places without realizing it was disconcerting to me.

So what if, I asked myself, one of my characters *always* finds herself waking up in strange and ridiculous places and has to adjust her life accordingly? And *voilà*—Suze Charles, sleepwalking heroine, was born.

And what better hero than a neurologist who specializes in sleep disorders? If he can't help her overcome her problem, she could be his worst nightmare. Also, how can she know if he loves her for herself or as a case study for the book he's writing?

Suze fosters animals that otherwise might not have another chance to be adopted. If you have the ability and an interest in fostering pets, go online and find a place near you that is looking for volunteers. Small acts of kindness and stewardship add up. You can make a difference for a pet and a family willing to adopt it.

That's how *Sleeping Beauty* came to be. I hope it makes you smile!

Blessings,

Judy

QUESTIONS FOR DISCUSSION

1. Do you or anyone you know have a sleeping disorder? How has it affected you?

2. Do you ever have crazy dreams that seem so real that you can hardly believe they were only in your head? How did they make you feel?

3. Have you ever found yourself in a situation as embarrassing as Suze Charles' when she's sleepwalking? What was it?

4. Have you ever known children like the Terror Twins? What do you think about parents who are too indulgent?

5. How did you feel Suze handled Tommy and Terry? Would you have done things differently.

6. What kind of life-style do you enjoy most— a cozy, whimsical home like Suze's or a contemporary place in the city? How easy would it be for you to adapt if you moved

from your current home to something that is just the opposite of what you've designed for yourself?

7. Suze fosters pets and gives them a final chance to find a home. Would you consider doing something like that?

8. Have you considered adopting a shelter animal? What would it take for you to do so?

9. Suze collects crazy things like mustache cups. Do you have a collection of something sentimental that doesn't make much sense to someone else? What is it?

10. Suze has a friend who wears a brightly colored Mohawk throughout most of the book. What do you think of a hairstyle like that? Would it color your judgment or opinion of the man wearing it?

HEARTWARMING INSPIRATIONAL ROMANCE

Contemporary,
inspirational romances
with Christian characters
facing the challenges
of life and love
in today's world.

**NOW AVAILABLE IN REGULAR
AND LARGER-PRINT FORMATS.**

Steeple
Hill®

Love Inspired SUSPENSE

RIVETING INSPIRATIONAL ROMANCE

Watch for our new series of
edge-of-your-seat suspense novels.
These contemporary tales
of intrigue and romance
feature Christian characters
facing challenges to their faith...
and their lives!

Steeple
Hill®

Visit:
www.SteepleHill.com